'Noah,' James said, placing a hand on Morgan's stiff back and urging her towards him. 'I don't know if you remember my sister Morgan?'

Since the memory of her naked is forever printed on my retina, I should think so.

Noah's mouth twitched, and when Morgan glared at him he thought that she'd worked out what he was thinking.

'Of course. Nice to see you again, Morgan,' he said, in his smoothest, blandest voice.

Wish you were naked, by the way.

'Noah,' Morgan said, and her eyes flicked over him, narrowed.

Noah just held her defiant stare. He'd perfected his implacable, don't-mess-with-me stare in the forces, and it had had more than a couple of recruits *and* higher-ranking officers buckling under. When Morgan started to flush he knew he had won their silent battle of wills. This time…

Dear Reader

So many children, bright and bold, are failed by the current schooling system because they don't fit into the 'academic' box society wants to shove them into. Over the years I've watched the struggles of a few dyslexic friends and the pain mothers of dyslexic children experience because school is a minefield for them. Because I believe that there are many different types of intelligence, and that one isn't better than another, I wanted to explore the effects dyslexia can have on an adult—especially one who comes from a wealthy, important and prominent family. Morgan, my bright, brave and bold heroine, is a result of those musings.

And Noah... Oh, I'm so in love with Noah. He's pulled himself out of a shocking family situation and is hard and tough, but he acts with integrity and honour. He's a sexy, reticent ex-SAS Scot who thinks he doesn't need anyone or anything. He probably doesn't...except Morgan. And he doesn't much like it.

Morgan and Noah are equally strong and equally vulnerable, and I so enjoyed getting to know them. I hope you will too!

With my best wishes

Joss

xxx

Come and say hi via
Facebook: Joss Wood Author,
Twitter: @josswoodbooks
or at www.josswoodbooks.com

FLIRTING WITH THE FORBIDDEN

BY
JOSS WOOD

MILLS
BOON

Published in Great Britain 2014
by Mills & Boon, an imprint of Harlequin (UK) Limited,
Eton House, 18-24 Paradise Road, Richmond, Surrey, TW9 1SR

© 2014 Joss Wood

ISBN: 978 0 263 24211 9

Joss Wood wrote her first book at the age of eight and has never really stopped. Her passion for putting letters on a blank screen is matched only by her love of books and travelling—especially to the wild places of Southern Africa—and possibly by her hatred of ironing and making school lunches.

Fuelled by coffee, when she's not writing or being a hands-on mum Joss, with her background in business and marketing, works for a non-profit organisation to promote the local economic development and collective business interests of the area where she resides. Happily and chaotically surrounded by books, family and friends, she lives in Kwa-Zulu Natal, South Africa, with her husband, children and their many pets.

Other Modern Tempted™ titles by Joss Wood:

THE LAST GUY SHE SHOULD CALL
TOO MUCH OF A GOOD THING
IF YOU CAN'T STAND THE HEAT…

This and other titles by Joss Wood are available in eBook format from www.millsandboon.co.uk

DEDICATION

*Vaughan and I have been married for twenty years
this year and he's my biggest fan,
my best friend and my favourite travelling companion.
He's also pretty hot...*

*This book is dedicated to him to say thanks
for making me coffee every morning,
for being a brilliant dad, for loving me so much
and for the fun that is our life.*

PROLOGUE

Eight years earlier...

NOAH FRASER LOOKED at the crown moulded ceilings above his head and tried not to think about the action in his pants—hmmm, at least he wasn't wearing a kilt. Truthfully, he could understand what was happening in his pants far more easily than he understood the mess in his head. Lust was easy, and there was a straightforward and time-honoured process for getting shot of it. But since the obvious was out of the question—it required a great deal more privacy than he currently had—he knew he had to distract himself.

He'd spent a lot of the past five years feeling horny—thanks to several tours of duty in dusty countries with little to no female interaction—and he'd learned a couple of techniques to relieve the frustration. Running through the process of dismantling his favourite weapon, the MP5 submachine gun, in the field usually did the trick.

Safety check. Check.

Noah banged his head back against the arm of the couch and cursed softly. What he really wanted was to get naked with that annoyingly sexy bundle of energy beyond the bedroom door. He was head-over-heels in *lust* with her...and a whole bunch of *like*. He could handle the lust...sorta, kinda... but the like had him tied up in knots.

It was a time of firsts for both of them. He was her first

bodyguard and hers was the first body—and what a body it was too!—he'd guarded. His mission was to keep her safe, and apparently hers was to crack the inscrutable façade he'd been told to present. It wasn't easy keeping his demeanour deadpan, because she was funny and smart and had a dry sense of humour that he deeply appreciated. He'd soon realised that she was winding him up by practising her flirting skills on him and it had started a battle of wills between them: she tried to get a reaction out of him and he refused to give her one. He still wasn't sure what the score was, but if they had to judge the competition by his frustration levels then she was streaks ahead.

Release bolt by vigorously slapping the cocking lever out of the indent. Check.

Okay, slight improvement…not much, but some. Noah, curled up on her too-small couch, glared at the closed door and cursed himself for being a fool…and for being unable to concentrate. Concentration, focus, control—control was his thing.

Pull out the locking pin…

His mind drifted again. She had the most amazing smile… and a 'shoot-all-the-blood-to-his-groin' body! Firm, toned, luscious, sweet…young.

Noah pulled the pillow over his head and silently screamed into the fabric. *Nineteen*, for crying out loud! He couldn't believe he was losing his mind over a teenager. He was a flippin' moron. Morgan Moreau was too young and she was his principal. His principal! Six months out of the unit, he was new to bodyguarding and the CFT Corporation, but he was pretty sure that sleeping with his principal was high up on the list of bodyguarding no-no's.

Since he had no intention of getting his ass fired over a piece of ass, no matter how sexy and tempting it was, he pulled the pillow away from his face, heaved in a deep breath and opened his eyes.

'Crap!' he yelled, scuttling up into the corner of the couch.

'Some bodyguard you are. I could've stabbed you in the heart,' Morgan drawled.

'You're naked,' Noah croaked, dimly aware that the saliva in his mouth had dried up. It had probably joined his blood as it sprinted south.

Naked, naked, naked, his body panted. *Yeah, baby!*

Noah was unable to stop his eyes from scanning her body. Perky breasts, a flat stomach, a Brazilian... Oh, he was a dead man...a Brazilian.

What was he thinking?

'You have amazing powers of observation,' Morgan said, her sexy mouth curving upwards. Her voice was perfect for the bedroom: gravelly, low, sexy.

'Why...? What...? How...?'

Morgan perched on the edge of the couch and placed her elbow on her knee, immensely at ease in her nakedness— which ratcheted up his level of panic. 'I thought you were brighter than that, Noah. I'm here, you're here—let's have some fun.'

Noah, his last two brain cells working overtime, narrowed his eyes at her. 'Subtle.'

'Straightforward,' Morgan countered. 'So, what do you say?'

They could... Who would know? They could have a couple of nights of uncomplicated sex, and when they'd hunted down the group of fanatics threatening her famous and wealthy family he'd return to the field and they could both move on with their lives. He'd move on to another job and she'd pull the same thing on another guy...

Noah frowned at the thought. While he believed in equality, the thought of Morgan getting naked with someone else left a sour taste in his mouth. It was on the tip of his tongue to warn her not to do this with anyone else, but he bit the words back.

Which was weird. He didn't like being controlled, hated people telling him what to do, so why did he want to do that to her? This was all too confusing; he'd had his fair share of sexual encounters but this was out of his ken. Way, *way* out. Outer Hebrides out.

He dropped his eyes to her chest and realised that she had the most amazing nipples—pink and succulent. All he had to do was reach for her arm and tumble her onto his lap. One little tug…

Nineteen. His job. Nineteen.

She was entrancing. Look at those eyes…the colour of bold green glass…

Nineteen. Job. Principal! He'd get his ass fired. Noah craned his neck and, yes, *her* ass was more gorgeous than he'd imagined.

Noah, as hard as stone, rolled to his feet and yanked his shirt up and over his head, thinking he'd get her to cover up, but instead he just stared at what she offered. Who would know? Truly, who would ever know?

His brain was back-pedalling, but he was facing a gorgeous naked girl who was offering herself on a plate, and the fact that he actually liked her as well was a nice bonus. When had he last genuinely *liked* a girl?

Walk away, Fraser, just walk away…

Then he remembered that he'd never had a halo that needed polishing.

Morgan felt his hand encircle her wrist, and as he launched her up into his hard body she closed her eyes in sheer, pure relief. For one moment she'd thought that this strong, quiet, sexy Scotsman was about to say no, that he was genuinely thinking about walking away. But suddenly he was hard under her hands, and his mouth on hers was an absolute revelation.

He kissed her as if he owned her, as if she was—just for this moment in time—his and only his. His mouth was hot, silky, sexy. Morgan felt his fingers digging into the skin on her hips and she wished that he would do something with them… Instead he just kissed her: long, liquid slides that tasted like heaven-coated sin.

Then Noah placed his hands under her butt and lifted her up and—oh, oh, *oh!*—onto his jeans-clad erection. The muscles in his arms bunched and she slid her hand up and down that tanned skin, briefly tracing the Celtic cross tattoo on his shoulder. Dropping her head, she kissed that smooth skin while he carried her back to her bedroom with an ease that astounded her.

A strong, sexy Scotsman… She couldn't believe that this was happening. Finally!

Noah lowered her down to the cool white sheets of her bed and loomed over her, his mouth going to her breast and pulling it into his mouth. Then he slid a hand between her legs and she arched off the bed as hot, sexual power pulsed through her. He slid a finger inside her and lifted his head to look into her face.

'So hot, so wet,' he muttered. 'You are a soldier's dream, lass.'

Morgan lifted her head and then smacked it against the bed as he built up a fire inside her that threatened to consume her.

'Can't believe I waited so long,' she growled to herself. 'Man, you're good at this.'

His finger stopped, his mouth pulled away from her breast and cool air drifted over her wet flesh. It was hot and muggy outside, but she knew that she'd crashed into an emotional iceberg.

'Sorry. I didn't mean to say that,' she muttered as he withdrew from her and rolled himself away.

'Were you hoping I wouldn't notice?'

'Kind of,' Morgan admitted.

He was trying to control himself; she could see that. He opened his mouth to say something and snapped his words back, his eyes sparking dangerously.

'So, how does this work? Did you decide that your virginity was something you no longer needed and I was handy?'

No! Yes! Kind of... How did she explain that she felt comfortable with him? Safe? From the moment she'd met him she'd known that he was authentic, solid. In her world, she didn't encounter those characteristics that often. He made her feel grounded, real...special.

And it didn't hurt that he had a hard, droolworthy body.

'I just thought...you...me...it would be fun.'

'Fun, huh?' Noah ran his hand through his hair and shook his head in disgust. 'Morgan, just what the hell do you think you're doing?'

'Why are you so angry?' Morgan demanded, pulling a sheet up and around her. Every inch of her skin was now blushing and she felt humiliated and confused. Why was this a problem? She was offering her body, not asking him to do her laundry.

'You don't just give it away—especially to someone like...' Noah trailed off. 'Damn it! Don't you have a boyfriend? Surely you've had offers? I see how those guys you hang out with look at you!'

Her blood cooled at the thought. 'None of them can keep their mouths shut and, trust me, my hooking up with someone would be huge news. And a very big feather in someone's cap.'

Since she hadn't slept with any of the society boys—sons of her mother's friends, acquaintances and connections— she knew that she was a fish to be hooked, a prize to be won. She wouldn't give any of those poncey, wishy-washy pseudo-men the satisfaction.

Noah looked ill—green—and Morgan's heart dropped like a brick. Only *she* could make a guy nauseous with an offer of sex.

'So you went trawling, huh?'

Trawling? Morgan frowned. Was he nuts? He was a far

better choice on any weekday and twice on Sundays. 'No, I— What's your problem anyway?'

'Just trying to figure out where I am in the pecking order. Above the pool boy but below the riding instructor? What comes next? Are you going to offer to pay me?'

Okay, now he was way off course. 'Stop being a jerk, Noah! Look, I like you, and I thought that you might like me...just a little. I thought that we were almost friends, and I'd rather do it with an almost-friend than someone who sees me as a prize.'

But Noah wasn't listening. He swore, his Scottish accent becoming rapidly more pronounced.. 'I knew this was a bad idea. What is *wrong* with me? I cannot believe that I let my libido override my common sense, my professionalism. Acting with integrity, my ass. She'd knock me into next year if she knew.'

Who? What on earth was he talking about?'

Noah shook his head as if to clear it and glowered at her. 'Put some clothes on. This isn't going to happen. Not now, not ever.'

Noah took one last look at her, then swore softly again as he turned and walked out of the room, slamming her bedroom door behind him.

Morgan winced and cursed the tears that stung her eyes. 'Guess that's a big old Scottish no, then.'

Curling into a ball, she lay on her bed and stared out through the open sash window. Sleep refused to come, and when she did manage to drift off she woke up to a stranger in her flat.

Noah had left and in his place was a female bodyguard— just in case, Morgan thought grimly, she was so desperate to get laid that she seduced the next male bodyguard who was assigned to her.

If losing her virginity had been the goal, then half the

population in the world could have sorted her out. But she didn't want half the population…

Stupid man; she wanted *him*.

CHAPTER ONE

NOAH FRASER DODGED past a couple kissing and ran his hand across his prickly jaw. His eyes flicked over the waiting crowds, mentally processing faces against his internal data bank, and nobody blipped on his radar until he saw a tall, thin man with his hands in the pockets of his expensive trousers.

He frowned and wondered what was so important that Chris had to meet him here.

Twenty hours ago he'd boarded a plane at the Ministro Pistarini International Airport just south of Buenos Aires, after a week spent doing a full-spectrum security analysis for a museum. He'd identified threats and risks and then provided them with solutions to plug the holes. It was a part of the business they were trying to grow and it was lucrative.

Because he was a frugal Scot, he still felt guilty that he'd upgraded his seat to business class, but he just hadn't been able to face the thought of wedging his six-foot-three frame into a minuscule economy class seat to spend thirteen hours in cramped misery. As Chris kept reminding him, business class also allowed him to review his files in privacy, to catch a couple of twenty-minute power naps, to drink good whisky. He'd worked hard for a long time, he told himself, and he—the business—could afford it.

Noah rolled his shoulders as he made his way through

Customs, looking forward to a decent shower, a beer and to sleeping for a week.

Of course sleeping for a week was a pipedream; he was working all hours of the day to build his company, and sleep was a luxury he just couldn't afford. Self-sufficiency and financial independence were a lot higher up on Noah's list of priorities than sleep.

Who knew why he was being met by Chris, his oldest friend, partner and second-in-command at Auterlochie Consulting? Something must be up. He swallowed as dread settled over him. The last time Chris had met him at the airport it had been because Kade, one of their best employees, had committed suicide. God, he didn't want to deal with something like *that* again…

'No one has died,' Chris said quickly and Noah wasn't surprised that he'd read his mind.

They'd learnt to read each other's faces—sometimes their thoughts—in dusty, unfriendly situations and it was a trait they'd never lost.

Noah did a minor eye-roll as Chris shook his hand and pulled him into that one-armed hug he did so well. Only Chris could get away with that kind of PDA; when you'd saved a guy's life you had to overlook his occasional sappiness.

Noah adjusted the rucksack on his shoulder as they made their way across the terminal. 'What's up?'

Chris jammed his hands in his pockets and gestured towards the nearest coffee shop. 'I'll explain. You look like hell.'

Noah grinned wryly. 'Nice to see you too.'

Ten minutes later Noah was slumped into a plastic seat at one of the many generic restaurants scattered throughout the hall. He sent his friend a sour look and took another sip of his strong black coffee. By his estimation he'd been awake for more than thirty hours and he was feeling punchy.

'How did the assessment go?' Chris asked.

'Brilliant. They took all my suggestions on board and paid the account via bank transfer before I left the office. The money should be through already.'

'It is. I checked. It's easy money, Noah.'

'And we can do it with our eyes closed. If we start getting a reputation for providing solid advice at a good price, I think we could double our turnover—and soon too.'

'We've already exceeded our initial projections for the business. In fact, we're doing really well.'

'We can do better. I want to build us into being the premier provider of VIP protection and risk assessment in the UK.'

'Not the world?' Chris quipped, gently mocking his ambition as he always did.

Chris was less driven than he was, and had his feet firmly placed on the ground. It wasn't a bad thing. Noah had enough ambition for both of them. They were great partners. Chris was better with people: he had an easy way about him that drew people in. Their clients and staff talked to Chris; he was their best friend, the elder brother, a mate. Chris was the touchy-feely half of their partnership.

Noah was tough, decisive and goal-orientated; the partner who kicked butt. He called it being disciplined, reasonable, responsible and dedicated in everything he did. Chris called it being a control freak perfectionist. And emotionally stunted. Yeah, yeah...

Well, that was what happened when you grew up far too fast... Noah ran a hand over his face as if to wipe away the memories of his childhood, of picking up the pieces when his mother died, the wrench of losing his brothers. He pulled in a breath and along with it control.

He *was* in control, he reminded himself. It was a long time ago that he was sixteen and had felt the earth shaking under his feet.

He saw Chris's insightful look and summoned up a smile. 'I've scheduled world domination for next year,' he quipped.

'What was the response when you told our employees that we wanted them to do a mandatory session with a psychologist every six months?'

'They grumbled, but they understood. Kade's death has rocked them all. You *do* know that we'll have to do it too.'

Noah blanched. 'Hell, no.'

'Hell, yes. Kade was our responsibility and we didn't pick up the signs. What if we're working too hard, trying to keep too many balls in the air, and we miss the signs in someone else? We have to be as mentally healthy as—*more* mentally healthy than—any of our employees, Noah. That's non-negotiable.'

Since Chris was the healthiest, most balanced person he knew, Noah didn't have to be a rocket scientist to know that Chris was talking about him. Chris thought he was too stressed—working like a demon, juggling far too many balls. He knew that Chris was worried about him burning out, but he also knew that that he was nowhere near the edge...

Working hard never killed anyone—and besides, he'd been to the edge before and he knew what it looked like. He was still miles away.

Chris slapped the folder he'd been holding onto the table and pushed it towards him. Flipping open the cover, Noah looked down into the laughing face of a green-eyed blonde. She was standing between her famous mother and father, her brother behind them. The most successful family on planet earth, he thought. Rich, successful, close. A unit.

He felt a pang of jealousy and told himself that despite the fact that he had not been part of his brothers' lives for most of their formative years he was now, and they weren't doing so badly.

Noah concentrated on the photo below him. Morgan... she'd grown up. She was wearing a tight, slinky cream dress that stopped inches below her butt and revealed her giraffe-long legs. Her blonde hair was pulled back into a smooth ponytail and her naturally made-up face was alight with joy. She looked fantastic. Happy, charismatic.

Hot.

Doing a stint as her bodyguard had nearly killed him. Apart from that one incident he'd never before or since needed the same amount of control and determination as he'd summoned the night he'd walked away from the gloriously naked Morgan Claire Morrisey Moreau.

Noah flipped through the papers in the file. 'Floor plans of the Forrester-Grantham hotel in New York. Photos of the Moreau jewellery collection… I thought the Moreaus were Amanda's clients—have always been CFT's clients?'

Amanda. Their ex-boss and his ex-lover. As petite and as dangerous as a black widow spider, she looked like every other ball-breaker businesswoman in the city.

Except that Amanda *actually* broke balls. She'd certainly tried to go for his when she'd found out that he was leaving the CFT Corporation to start a company that was in direct competition with hers.

That hadn't been a day full of fun and giggles.

'Well, as you know, James Moreau and I went to school together,' Chris said.

Noah shrugged off his tiredness to connect the dots. James Moreau: CEO of Moreau International, brother to Morgan and son to Hannah 'Queen of Diamonds' Moreau and Jedd Moreau, one of the world's best known geologists.

Moreau International owned diamond and gemstone mines, dealt in the trading of said gems—especially diamonds—and had exclusive jewellery stores in all the major cities around the world. Hannah, as the face of the company, had always been a target, and CFT routinely provided her and Jedd with additional bodyguards when they needed more protection than their long-term driver/guards. That protection was only extended to James and Morgan and other high-ranking executives within MI when MI's security division or CFT received a particular threat, or were monitoring a situation where extra protection was needed.

Eight years ago, just after he'd left the SAS, Noah had been unlucky enough to end up guarding the nineteen-year-old Morgan for a week because a well-funded but stupid militant environmental group had been protesting MI's involvement with mines in a nature reserve in Uganda. Huge threats had been issued until it had been pointed out that it was an oil company mining for natural gas and not MI looking for gems.

Morgan had never been in any real danger, but no one had been prepared to take the chance. As the rookie, he'd got the so-called 'creampuff' assignment to guard the teenager. He'd never told anyone that it had probably been one of the best weeks of his life. Sure, he'd vacillated between wanting to wring her neck and fantasising about her, which had been off-the-scale inappropriate since she'd been his principal and he'd been six years older than her—and a million years in experience. But he'd laughed—internally—been relaxed in her company and had enjoyed her scalpel-sharp mind.

Noah felt heat creep up his neck and he stared at the fingers that gripped his coffee cup. He'd lost his mind that night...well, almost. He'd nearly risked everything he had—his sole source of income at that time—to make love to her. The consequences of his actions still made his blood run cold. If CFT had found out he would have been canned and would never have been able to get another job in security again. And security was what he did—what he'd trained for—the only skill he'd had at that time.

He'd left the army, his first and only love, to find a better-paying job so that he could put his two younger brothers through college. CFT had offered him a fantastic salary which he'd nearly thrown away to sleep with Morgan Moreau.

Who'd just wanted him to break her duck!

Chris's voice pulled him back to the here and now. 'I've

been working on James to send some business our way, told him we've expanded into security analysis, and he's thrown us a bone.'

'Oh, yay,' Noah deadpanned.

'If we pull it off it gives us an in at Moreau and we want them as clients.' Chris reminded him. 'World domination, remember? Moreau's is a good place to start.'

'I know, I know... Okay, what is it?' He tapped Morgan's picture. 'Does she need a bodyguard again? Who has her family upset this time?'

'She doesn't need protection.'

'Good.' Noah lifted an eyebrow at Chris. 'What's the job?'

'Every five years the Moreaus host a grand ball for charity, and they combine the ball with an exhibition of the family collection of jewels—which is practically priceless. Some of the biggest and the best diamonds and jewels collected over generations of wealthy Moreaus,' Chris explained. 'There has been a massive increase in armed robberies at such jewellery exhibitions, and James wants a complete, intensive threat analysis. I know it's a puffball assignment, but you just need to head to New York for a meeting, have a look at their current security arrangements, check out the hotel—do what you do best. With luck we'll get the contract to oversee the security, based on your report. But for now, it's just a couple of days in New York and we have an in with Moreau.'

'When is this meeting?'

'In the morning. I have you booked on a flight leaving in an hour.'

'Why can't you go? You're James's mate, not me.' Noah groaned. 'I'm beat.'

'I've got a meeting scheduled with another client, and you are far better at security assessments than I am. You're brilliant at planning operations, getting in and out of places and situations you shouldn't be, and you can see stuff from a criminal perspective.'

'Thanks,' Noah said dryly.

Noah pushed his chair out and stretched his long legs. He linked his hands behind his head in his favourite thinking posture, his eyes on Morgan's photograph which lay between them on the grubby table. Gorgeous eyes and slanting cheekbones, and she had a wide, mobile mouth with a smile that could power the national electrical grid.

Noah licked his lips and forced his thoughts away from that dangerously sexy mouth. Slowly he raised his eyes to Chris's face. He leaned forward and rested his arms on the table. 'Why don't you just shoot me now?'

'It's an option, but then I'd be out of a partner. It's a few days, Noah, in an exciting city that you love.'

'Clothes?'

'Bag in the car. I went to your flat and picked out some threads.'

Noah swore and flipped the cover of the folder closed. 'Guess I'm going to New York.'

'Atta boy.'

Noah narrowed his eyes at his partner. 'You're a manipulative git.'

Chris just grinned.

Sapphires, rubies, pearls. Diamonds. The usual suspects. And then there were the less common gems that sparked her imagination. Alexandrite that changed from green in daylight to red under incandescent light. Maw Sit-Sit, the same green as her eyes. Almandine Garnet, purplish red and the neon blue of Paraiba tourmaline.

Having access to the gemstone vaults of Moreau International was a very big perk as a jewellery designer, and it allowed Morgan the chance to offer her very high-end clients one-of-a-kind pieces containing gemstones of exceptional quality.

Morgan looked up at Derek, their Head of Inventory, and the security guard who'd accompanied the jewels to her airy, light-filled design studio on the top floor of the

Moreau Building on Fifth Avenue from the super-secure fourth floor that housed the jewellery vaults. Morgan knew that there was another vault somewhere in the city, and others in other places of the world, which housed more gemstones. Her mother didn't believe in keeping all their precious eggs in one basket.

'I'll take the Alexandrite, the tourmaline and both garnets.' Morgan scanned the cloth holding the jewels again. 'The fifteen-carat F marquise-cut yellow diamond and I'll let you know about the emeralds. Thanks, Derek.'

Derek nodded and stepped forward to help Morgan replace the jewels in their separate bags. She signed an order form as Derek spoke.

'I have some apparently amazing Clinohumite coming in from a new mine in Siberia. Interested?'

Interested in the rare burnt orange gems that she could never get enough of? *Duh*. 'Of course! I'll owe you if you can sneak a couple of the nicer ones to me before you offer them to Carl.'

Carl was Head Craftsman for MI's flagship jewellery store which was on the ground floor of the building. A rival to Tiffany and Cartier, Moreau's made up the third of the 'big three' jewellery stores in New York City. Carl had his clients and so did Morgan, and they shared one or two others. They happily waged a silent war, competing for the best of the Moreau gems that were on offer. And for the clients with the deepest pockets.

'I'll offer you two per cent above whatever Carl offers for the Clinohumites. Don't let me down, Derek, I want those stones.' She might be a Moreau, but her business was separate to the jewellery store and the gemstones. She had to buy her stones at the going rate and sell at a profit...and that was the way she liked it.

'Of course. I owe you for designing Gail's engagement ring. She still thinks I'm a god.'

Morgan laughed. 'I'm glad she loves it.'

Even though he had a hugely responsible job at Moreau's, he would never have been able to afford the usual prices Morgan commanded. Sometimes she thought that the money she charged for her designs was insane but, as her mother kept insisting, exclusivity had its price, and the Moreau price was stratospheric.

Morgan heard the door to her studio click closed behind Derek and his guard and sat down on a stool, next to her workbench. She twisted a tanzanite and diamond ring on her finger before resting her chin in the palm of her hand.

Morgan Moreau Designs. She couldn't deny that being a Moreau had opened doors that would have been a lot harder to break down if she hadn't possessed a charmed name associated with gemstones. But having a name wasn't enough; no socialite worth her salt was going to drop squillions on a piece of jewellery that wasn't out of the very top drawer. Morgan understood that they wanted statement pieces that would stand out from the exceptional, and she provided that time and time again.

It was the one thing—probably the only thing—she'd ever truly excelled at. She adored her job; it made her heart sing. So why, then, exactly, wasn't she happy? Morgan twisted her lips, thinking that she wasn't precisely unhappy either. She was just...feeling 'blah' about her life.

Which was utterly ridiculous and she wanted to slap herself at the thought. She was a Moreau—wealthy, reasonably attractive, popular. She ran her own business and had, if she said so herself, a great body which didn't need high maintenance. Okay, she was still single, and had been for a while—her soul mate was taking a long time to make an appearance—but she dated. Had the occasional very discreet affair if she thought the man nice enough and attractive enough to bother with.

She had a life that millions of girls would sell their souls for and she was feeling sorry for herself? *Yuck.*

'Earth to Morgan?'

Morgan looked up and saw her best friend standing in the doorway of her studio, her pixie face alight with laughter. Friends since they were children, they'd lived together, travelled together and now they worked together...sort of. Riley was contracted to design and maintain the window displays of the jewellery store downstairs. She was simply another member of the Moreau family.

'Hey. I'm about to have coffee—want some?'

Riley shook her head. 'No time. Your mother sent me up here to drag you out of your nest. She wants you to come down and join the charity ball planning meeting.'

'Why? She's never included me before.'

'You know that's not true. Every year she asks if you want to be involved, and every year you wrinkle your pretty nose and say no.'

'You'd think she would've got the message by now,' Morgan grumbled. Organising an event on such a scale was a mammoth undertaking and *so* not up her alley. She'd just make an idiot of herself and that wasn't an option. Ever.

She'd felt enough of an idiot far too many times before.

'Well, she said that I have to bring you down even if I have to drag you by your hair.'

'Good grief.'

Morgan stood up and stretched. She took stock of her outfit: a white T-shirt with a slate jacket, skinny stone-coloured pants tucked into black, knee-high laceup boots. It wasn't the Moreau corporate look, but she'd do.

Morgan walked towards the door and allowed it to close behind her; like all of the other rooms in the building, entrance was by finger-scan. Keys weren't needed at Moreau's.

'Did you get your dress for Merri's wedding?' Riley asked as they headed for the stairs.

'Mmm. I can't wait. We're hitching a lift with James on the company jet, by the way. He's flying out on the Thursday evening.'

'Perfect.'

And it was… Their friend Merri was getting married in her and Riley's hometown of Stellenbosch, South Africa, and Morgan couldn't wait to go home. She desperately missed her home country; she'd love to return to the vineyards and the mountains, the crisp Cape air and the friendly people. But if she wanted to cement her reputation for being one of the best jewellery designers in the world—like her grandfather before her—then she needed to be in fast-paced NYC. She needed clients with big money who weren't afraid to spend it…

And talking of exceptional, she thought as they stepped out of the lift onto the fifth floor, where Hannah and the New York-based directors of MI had their offices, she had to start work on the piece Moreau International had commissioned her to design and manufacture that would be sold as part of the silent auction at the charity ball. Maybe that was why Hannah wanted her at the meeting…

CHAPTER TWO

MORGAN WATCHED AS her glamorous, sophisticated mother stepped out of her office in a lemon suit, nude heels and with a perfectly straight platinum chin-length bob.

'I need a decision about the jewellery for the auction,' Morgan announced as Hannah approached them. 'Do you have any gemstones in stock that you want me to use? What do you want me to design? Diamonds? Emeralds? Rubies? Classic or contemporary? Is that why you want me at this meeting?'

'Hello to you too, darling,' Hannah said in her driest tone. 'How are you?'

Morgan waved an elegant hand in the air. 'Mum, we had coffee together this morning; you didn't say anything then about me having to come downstairs.'

'It's a conference room, not a torture chamber, Morgan,' Hannah replied, her tone as dry as the martinis she loved to drink. 'Nice photo of you in the *Post*, by the way.'

Since she hadn't been out recently, Morgan wasn't sure where she'd been photographed. 'Uh...where was I?'

'At the opening night of that new gallery in Soho.'

Her friend Kendall's new gallery; she'd popped in for five minutes, literally, and it couldn't go undocumented? *Sheez!* But she was, very reluctantly, a part of the NYC social scene, and because she was a Moreau whenever she made an appearance she was photographed extensively. Many of those photographs ended up in the social columns and online.

Hannah folded her arms and tapped her foot. Good grief, she recognised that look.

'Morgan, it's time we talked about you joining Moreau International in an official position.'

Morgan sighed. 'Has six months passed so quickly?'

They had an agreement: Hannah was allowed to nag her about joining the company every six months. For the last twelve years they'd had the same conversation over and over again.

'I've decided that I want you to be MI's Public Relations and Brand Director.'

Run me over with a bus, Morgan thought. PR and Brand Director? That was a new title. 'Mum, I'm happy doing what I'm doing—designing jewellery. You and James are doing a fabulous job with MI. You don't need me.'

And she was damned if she was going to take a job away from a loyal MI employee who was way more qualified for the position than she'd ever be. And—funny, this—she actually wanted to get paid for what she *did*, not who she was.

But she had to give Hannah points for being persistent. She'd been trying to get her to work for MI since she was sixteen—shortly after they'd received the happy news that Morgan was just chronically dyslexic and not selectively stupid.

It had only taken her mother and a slew of medics, educational psychologists and shrinks to work that out. Everyone had been so pleased that they'd found the root cause of her failing marks at school, her frustration and her anger.

The years of sheer hell she'd lived through between the time she'd started school and her diagnosis had been conveniently forgotten by everybody except herself.

Water under the bridge, Morgan reminded herself. And she knew her mum felt guilty for the part she'd played in the disaster that had been her education.

Morgan knew that it hadn't been easy for her either. She'd

been thrust into running MI in her mid-thirties, when her adventure-seeking husband had decided that he didn't like the corporate life and wanted to be MI's chief geologist, discovering new mines. Hannah, with her MBA in business and economics, had taken over the role of MI's CEO, juggling its huge responsibilities with two children, one of whom had made her life a great deal more difficult by her inability to meet her mother's and teachers' expectations.

How often had she heard variations on the theme of, 'She's such a bright child; if only she would try harder.'

Nobody had ever realised how hard she'd always been trying, how incredibly frustrating it had been not to meet her goals and everybody else's. Had they honestly believed that she didn't want to learn to read and write properly? That she'd enjoyed being the class freak?

Ages eight to sixteen had been a suck-fest of epic proportions. Finally being diagnosed as being chronically dyslexic had freed her, a little, from the shame and guilt she'd felt for years. She'd started to believe that her learning disabilities weren't her fault and her relationship with her family—well, mostly with her mother—had rapidly improved. Her mum was still a controlling corporate queen, and she still marched to the beat of her own drum, but they'd found a way back to each other—even if they did have to have this conversation every six months.

Morgan knew that she wasn't stupid, but she also knew that working for MI would require computers and reading and writing reports. While she *could* do all of that, she just took longer than most—okay, a lot longer—and the corporate world couldn't and wouldn't wait that long. And shouldn't...

Until she was the best person for a job, she wouldn't take it. Not to mention that her dyslexia would become an open secret; she wouldn't be able to keep it under wraps. Wouldn't that be fun? She could just see the headlines: *The ultimate dumb blonde... Gorgeous but thick... With her looks and money, who needs brains anyway?*

She'd heard them all before—even from someone she'd loved…

Morgan shuddered. *No, thank you.* Call her stubborn, call her proud, but she wasn't going to expose herself to that much ridicule again.

Besides, designing jewellery was her solace and her joy— her dream job. If only Hannah would see that and get off her back about working for MI her relationship with her mum would be pretty much perfect.

Morgan took her mum's hand and squeezed. 'I love you for the fact that you believe I should play a bigger part in MI, but I am neither qualified nor suited for the corporate world, Mum. I don't *want* to be part of that world. I'm happy being on the fringes of MI.'

'I will wear you down someday.' Hannah sighed loudly. 'On another subject, I want you to haul out your designer dresses and start creating hype around the ball at social events.'

Morgan gagged. '*Ugh.* Don't I do enough already?'

'Hardly.' Hannah sniffed. 'One function every two weeks and cutting out early isn't good enough to promote your business, and not nearly good enough to promote the ball. You need to charm more people than you're currently doing. Darling, you are a social disgrace. How many invitations did you turn down this week alone?'

Morgan shrugged. 'Ten…twelve?'

'Helen, my personal publicist, said that you were invited to at least twenty-five, maybe more. Soirées, charity dinners, afternoon teas, breakfasts…'

Morgan tipped her head and counted to ten, then thirty, before attempting to speak rationally. 'Mum, I have a business to run, designs to get out the door. I work, just like you do. Okay, I don't oversee a multinational company but I work. Hard.'

'You're a Moreau; you should be out more. Can you start going to some more formal parties? The benefits, the politi-

cal fundraisers, the balls? That is where the money is, darling—the people who can actually afford the price of the
ball tickets. We need to target the people who have the *real*
money, and they are at the more sedate functions.'

Sedate meaning deadly dull. 'Don't nag me, Mother. You
know I hate those stuffy functions where the conversation is
so...intense. The situation in Syria, the economy, the plight
of the rainforests.'

'Because, you know, those issues *aren't* important...'
Riley said, her tongue in her cheek.

Morgan glared at her. 'I feel...' She wanted to say *stupid*
but instead said, 'I feel out of place there.'

Like all the other issues related to her dyslexia, it had
taken her many years to conquer her social awkwardness and
to decode social cues. She still battled with new situations,
and she knew that many people took her occasional lapses
of concentration and her social shyness as self-absorption
and disinterest. Nothing could have been further from the
truth. She generally loved people, but she could never tell if
they loved her back.

When she added that to her 'I wonder if he sees me or
just the family money' concerns, dating was a bit of a nightmare...

And, really, she would rather have a beer in a pub in jeans
and a T-shirt than be in a ballroom in shoes that hurt her feet.

Riley smiled at her and Morgan recognised the mischie-
vous glint in her eyes.

'You poor child...being forced to dress up, drink the best
champagne in the world and eat the finest food at functions
that are by invitation only. It's almost abuse—really, it is.'

Morgan's searing look promised retribution for Riley's
teasing and her encouragement of her mother's campaign to
get her to be the reigning young socialite of New York City.

Morgan wrinkled her nose at her mother. 'You and James
just do it so much better than me. You're suave and sophisticated and far more charming than I'll ever be—with or with-

out the big D. Look, we've discussed my contribution to the ball so can I go now?' Morgan asked hopefully.

'No, I'd still like you to attend this first planning meeting with Riley, Jack—our PR director—and the new consultant James has appointed to assess security,' Hannah said as they walked down the carpeted passage to the boardroom.

On the walls either side were framed photographs of the Moreau collection of jewels.

'Why can't Moreau's own Chief of Security handle it? He always has,' Morgan said, because she felt she should show *some* interest.

'Since the last Moreau ball there have been a number of armed robberies on jewellery exhibitions.' Hannah rapped her fist against the frame that held a picture of the Moreau Diamond—a gem Morgan's three times great-grandfather Moreau had bought from a broke Russian aristocrat and which had once been owned by Elizabeth of Russia. 'Fifty-three carats, D-colour, flawless. Worth more than five million dollars. You want to risk it getting stolen?'

When she put it like that…

'Our jewellery collection is priceless, Morgan, so James has contracted Auterlochie Consulting to look at every security hole we have and to plug it. Their best operative will be in charge…'

Auterlochie…Auterlochie… Why did she know that name?

'In you go, darling, and smile!'

Hannah placed a hand on her back and she bared her teeth at her mother as she stepped into the conference centre. Her hand still on the doorknob, she looked around—and her head jerked back as dazzling blue eyes connected with hers.

Deep brown hair… Auterlochie… A deep Sean Connery voice explaining that it was a town in the Scottish Highlands, situated on a loch, and he'd once visited it with a friend. Two young boys had fished and explored the icy banks there, and he'd told her when he opened his business it would be called Auterlochie something.

It was the one of the longest sentences he'd strung together, and Morgan had been enthralled by his Scottish accent and the light of determination in those fantastic cobalt eyes... Noah Fraser.

Morgan's heart splattered as it hit the floor. *Bats on a broomstick.*

She stepped back behind the door and squeezed her eyes shut. Eight years and she still wished she could acid-wash the memory out of her brain.

'Excuse me. I really need to go to the bathroom.'

'Oh, Morgan? Right now? The meeting...'

Hannah's voice followed her down the hall.

In the upscale visitors' bathroom where she'd fled after Hannah had dropped her verbal meteor strike, Morgan sat on the lid of a toilet and stared at her hands. She knew she had to get moving, get to the meeting, or her mum would hunt her down like a rabid fox but she didn't know if she could face Noah Fraser again.

She'd rather flush herself down the toilet bowl.

'Morgs?' A fist rapped on the door. 'You in there? Your mum is *not* a happy camper.'

Morgan leaned forward and flipped the lock to open. Riley pulled the door open and frowned. She sent her a pointed look. 'Why are you hiding out in the bathroom?'

Morgan bit the inside of her cheek. 'Did you meet Noah Fraser?'

'The security guy? Yes. Very intense, very hot.'

Morgan swore and dropped her face to her hands.

'And the problem is...?'

Morgan briefly explained her history with Noah and Riley lifted her hands in confusion. 'So you made a move on the guy and he said no? It was a long time ago, Morgan.'

Morgan knew that if there was anyone who would understand what she was about to say Riley was it. They'd been friends forever and she had witnessed Morgan's constant struggles with the system. Shortly after the incident with Noah she'd moved in as Morgan's flatmate. Riley had watched her struggle through college to get her diploma in Gemology and Jewellery Design—it had taken her double the time to get as anyone else, even with a scribe—and she knew the challenges she faced on a daily basis and had supported her through the hard times.

'Okay, I need more details. So tell me about Mr Melt-My-Panties. And hurry up—your mother is going to have both our hides soon.'

'When I was nineteen the parents had some kidnapping threats made against them by some weird group and Noah was assigned as my bodyguard.'

'Uh-huh...'

'After a week of hanging with him I threw myself at him—actually, I threw my *naked* self at him.' Morgan nodded at Riley's wince. 'He kissed me, discovered I was a virgin, and then he declined the offer. I was so humiliated. I liked him—felt so at ease with him despite the fact that he hardly spoke—and his rejection felt like—'

'Like what, hon?'

'I can't explain it, and I don't know why, but his rejection made me feel swamped with shame. Every emotion I'd ever experienced with my dyslexia—the lack of self-belief, the fear of judgement—dropped on me like a ton of bricks. It was horrible. He made me feel worthless again. And now is not the time to tell me that nobody can make me *feel* worthless!'

'Okay. No lectures. Did he know that you were dyslexic?'

'No, I was very careful to keep it from him. For that summer I was Morgan without the big D. That's what made it even harder, I think... He rejected me anyway. Around him I was the most normal I had ever been and it still wasn't enough. I still can't think of that night without feeling cold and clammy.'

'Oh, honey... Well, you know you're not worthless. You've worked hard to climb out of that pit of feeling *less than* and not valued. Why are you letting those feelings, and that man, chase you into a bathroom stall? You're better than that.'

She *was*, dammit. 'I know that...' she muttered.

'Then get your butt out of there and pick up your chin. You'll be fine. Me, I'm not so sure.' Riley wiggled her butt.

Morgan lifted her hands in query. 'What's the matter with you?'

'I think my panties are starting to melt...can I hit on him?'

'Sheez, Ri!' Morgan snapped. 'No, you can't hit on him! I mean, yes, you can... *Aarrgh!*'

Riley's chuckles followed her out of the bathroom.

This time he'd sent *her* running.

Judging from her hasty retreat and her *oh, crap!* look, nobody had told her he would be at the meeting. While he hadn't expected Morgan to attend this meeting, at least he'd been prepared to run into her. And he'd had a six hour flight to practise his *oh-it's-you* face.

He understood her belting out of the room; he'd fought the same impulse himself. That and the inclination to grab her and pick up where they'd left off years ago. She'd be naked, of course...

Noah looked down at the table he was sitting at and concentrated hard. Thirty-three years old and he was grateful that his crotch was hidden from view by a sleek boardroom table.

Get a grip, Fraser. Distraction... Years ago he'd used firearm drills; now he just flipped open his iPad and checked his emails. Ten minutes later he glanced at his watch and stifled a frustrated sigh. The meeting still hadn't started.

He'd made Morgan run off screaming into the... Well, not the night, but he still couldn't blame her. It wasn't his finest memory and *he* hadn't been naked...with a Brazilian... *Do not go there, Fraser.*

He glanced over to the corner, where Hannah Moreau and her son James, who'd just entered the conference room, were standing. He'd met James once before, and despite the fact that he was one of the richest men in the world he rather liked the guy. He was smart, decisive, and didn't give off an air of being precious.

He also knew, from Chris, that he played a cracking game of touch rugby, didn't play polo, and could talk to miners and millionaires with equal ease. He couldn't help hoping that Morgan had turned out equally well.

Not that he cared—much—one way or the other.

Noah saw the conference door open and didn't realise that he'd sucked in his breath. The arty-looking redhead stepped through the door first, and exchanged a look with James that was part defiance, part attraction—something cooking there—and then Noah focused his attention on the figure in the doorway.

'Sorry I kept you waiting, everybody. Hi, James.'

James Moreau whirled around and immediately crossed the room, pulling Morgan into his embrace. Morgan's butterscotch-coloured head rested on his chest and she closed her eyes as she returned the hug. When she opened them again she looked straight at him—now utterly composed—with those clear, deep green eyes, and it was his turn to feel something akin to exposed and vulnerable…as if she'd cracked him open and his every thought, emotion, fear was there for her to read.

In another reality—the one where he wasn't losing his mind—Noah remembered his manners and forced himself to his feet, taking a moment to pull his thoughts together and to display his usual expression. He called it inscrutable; Chris called it bored indifference. He pulled in a shallow breath and made himself relax while Morgan shook hands with the others in the room. He watched her interact and knew that her smile wasn't as wide as it could be, that the muscles in her slim shoulders were taut with tension, that she was trying to delay the moment of having to acknowledge his presence.

Well, he wasn't entranced with the idea either. Entranced with *her*, yes. With the reality of being entranced by her…no.

He didn't do entranced.

'Noah,' James said, placing a hand on Morgan's stiff back and urging her towards him, 'I don't know if you remember my sister Morgan?'

Since the memory of her naked is forever printed on my retina, I should think so.

Noah's mouth twitched, and when Morgan glared at him he thought that she'd worked out what he was thinking. 'Of course. Nice to see you again, Morgan,' he said, in his smoothest, blandest voice.

Wish you were naked, by the way.

'Noah,' Morgan said. Her eyes flicked over him, narrowed, and then she gave him a 'you're a bug and I'm desperate to squash you' look.

What was her problem? He hadn't asked her to proposition him… Was she still annoyed because he'd said no? *Come on, it was eight years ago—get over it, already.*

Noah held her defiant stare. He'd perfected his own implacable, don't-mess-with-me stare in the forces, and it had had more than a couple of recruits and higher-ranking officers buckling under. When Morgan started to flush he knew had he won their silent battle of wills. This time.

'Take a seat everyone.'

Noah turned back to the table and pulled out the chair next to him for Morgan, gestured her into it. She narrowed her eyes at him, yanked it back another couple of inches in a flouncy display of defiance and dropped into it. Noah could smell her scent, something light and fresh, and felt a rush of blood heading south, making him feel almost light-headed. She still wore the same perfume and it transported him back to that night so long ago, when he'd tangled with temptation and by the skin of his teeth escaped.

'Right, the first item of business…' Hannah said, in a crisp, no-nonsense voice when they were all seated and looking at her expectantly. 'I'm handing over the responsibility of the ball to you, Morgan, and it's not under discussion. Make me proud.'

CHAPTER THREE

WHEN SHE WAS very tired, stressed or emotional Morgan saw dots in front of her eyes and the letters on a page danced and shuffled about. However, this was the first time the room had ever moved, that faces had bopped and objects jiggled.

Morgan closed her eyes and wondered if she had imagined the last thirty seconds. She'd thought she'd heard her mother say that she wanted her to take over the organising the Moreau Charity Ball—the most anticipated ball on the international social scene, held once every five years, displaying the full collection of gemstones and jewellery the Moreau family had acquired over many generations.

There were only three thousand guests attending, five hundred of whom were invited by Hannah herself from among their loyal customers, long-time business associates and preferred suppliers. For the rest, whether they were royalty or the average Joe, they had to place a bid for a double ticket and the highest bids won the highly sought after tickets.

It was outrageous how much people were prepared to pay for a double ticket. Simply inconceivable... And that was why, along with the auction, the Moreau Charity Ball raised tens of millions for the various causes they supported around the world.

But for their money their guests expected the best entertainers, visually stunning dress sets, Michelin star quality food—the whole gilt-plated bang-shoot.

It was rich, it was exclusive, it was the social highlight of the half-decade. And if you wanted to be part of the experience then you paid, stratospherically, for the privilege of being there.

And Hannah wanted *her* to run it? Morgan felt her throat constrict. She lifted her left hand and didn't realise that she was groping for Noah's hand until his strong fingers encircled her palm and squeezed.

'Breathe,' he told her, his voice authoritative even though it was pitched at a volume only she could hear. 'Again; in and out. There you go.'

Morgan felt the room settle as oxygen reached her brain and lungs. When she thought she could speak she licked her lips and considered removing her hand from Noah's strong grasp. But since it seemed to be her only tenuous link to reality, she left it exactly where it was.

Morgan made herself look at her mother, who had the slightest smile on her face. 'Is this a joke?'

'Not at all,' Hannah replied. 'I'd like you to plan, organise and execute the ball.'

'But—'

'Riley will help you with the creative side—help you pick the theme, do the design. You both have an amazing streak of creativity and I know that it will look visually spectacular.'

Morgan shook her head, wishing she could speak freely and say exactly what was on her mind. *I don't do well with reading reports, writing reports, analysing spreadsheets. You know this! I've worked really hard to conquer my dyslexia, but it's still there and it becomes a lot worse when I'm stressed. This ball will stress me out to the max! I don't want to mess this up; it's too important for me to be in charge of.*

Hannah's eyes softened but determination radiated from her face. 'Honey, I know that you will be fine. I know that you also have your own commissions, your own business to run, so the full resources that are available to me are available to you too. We'll hire you a PA for this project; she'll type your reports and be your general gopher. James will keep an eye on the finances and you'll liaise with Jack regarding the promotion and advertising of the ball. Noah will draw up plans to keep the jewels safe, and I'll be on the other end of a mobile. You just have to co-ordinate, make decisions, boss people about.'

'You're good at that,' James inserted with an easy grin.

And in a couple of sentences her mother, without announcing to the room that she had a problem reading and writing, waved away her biggest concerns.

Morgan reluctantly pulled her hand out from Noah's and flushed, because she could sense those deep blue eyes on her face. What must he think of her? she wondered. That she was a candidate for an upmarket loony bin?

'Why are you bowing out, Hannah?' Riley asked, as forthright as ever.

Hannah picked up her pen and tapped the point on the stack of papers in front of her. Morgan saw a quick, secret smile on her face and frowned. It was a good question, and one she was sure she knew the answer to... Three, two, one...

'I need a break—to step away from the business for a while.'

There it is and here we go again... Morgan thought. Now they were getting to the bottom of things. Every ten years or so her parents decided that they should try and live together again. They loved each other, but they loved each other more when they had continents between them. They refused to accept that while they adored each other they just couldn't live together. How many times had her father moved in and out of the Stellenbosch farmhouse and, later, the Englewood mansion?

Morgan sent James a quick eye-roll and he responded with a faint smile.

'Jedd and I have realised that we've been married nearly forty years and we want to spend more time with each other. He's going to try to be a little less of a mad geologist and I'm going to accompany him on his travels. So I need you, Morgan, to organise the ball for me.'

Morgan expelled her pent-up tension in a long stream of air. If this was about her parents' marriage then she gave her mum a week and she'd be on the company jet back home. Hannah couldn't go five minutes without checking her email or applying her lipstick. Her father spent weeks in jungles without making contact, sleeping in tents and hammocks and, she suspected, not washing much.

A week, maybe two, and Hannah would be back and yanking the ball's organisation into her beautifully mani-cured hands. Fine by her. She just had to ride it out.

What a morning, Morgan thought. Noah, the ball, her parents; she felt as if she was in sensory and information overload.

'Right, down to business,' Hannah said sharply.

Morgan frowned and held up her hand. 'Whoa! Hold on, there, Mum.' Morgan narrowed her eyes at her beautiful, wilful mother. If she gave her mother an inch, she'd gobble her up. 'I will sit in on this first planning meeting and then I will decide how involved I want to become—because I know that you will whirl back in here in two weeks' time and take over again.'

Blue eyes held green and Hannah's mouth eventually twitched with a smile. She nodded, looked around the table and pulled on her cloak of business. 'Okay. Now, we've wasted enough time on our family drama. Back to work, everyone.'

By the end of the two-hour meeting Morgan felt as if her head was buzzing. She desperately needed a cup of coffee and some quiet. Just some time to think, to process, to deal with the events of the morning.

She wanted to run up to her studio, lie down on her plush raspberry love seat and just breathe. But instead, because Hannah had asked her super-nicely, she was accompanying Noah to the Forrester-Grantham Hotel—the oldest, biggest and most beautiful of Manhattan's hotels. It had the only ballroom in New York City big enough to accommodate the ball's many guests, and the fact that it was lush, opulent and a six-star venue made it their instinctive hotel of choice.

Morgan had been delegated, by her mother, to introduce Noah to the hotel's Head of Security and discuss the current security arrangements for the ball.

Yippee.

Riley, the last to leave, closed the door behind her and Morgan was left alone with Noah. She watched as he unfurled his long body and headed for the refreshment table in the corner. He placed a small cup beneath the spout of the coffee machine and hit the button marked 'espresso'. He was different, Morgan thought. His body, under that nice grey suit, still seemed to be as hard as it had been eight years ago, but his hair was longer, his face thinner. Okay, he was older, but what felt so different? Maybe it was because now he radiated determination, a sense of power...leaving no one in doubt that he was a smart, ambitious man in his prime.

Noah snagged two bottles of sparkling water from the ice bucket, held them loosely in one hand as he picked up the small cup and brought it back to the table. To her surprise, he slid the cup and a bottle towards her.

'You look like you need both,' Noah said, pushing away the chair next to her with his foot and resting his bottom on the conference table so that he faced her. He picked up a bottle of water, twisted the cap off and took a long sip.

Morgan lifted the cup to her lips, swallowed and tipped her head so that it rested against the high back of the leather chair. Her mind skittered over all the questions she wanted to ask him: where did he live? He wasn't wearing a ring but was he married? Involved? Why had he said no to her all those years ago?

She opened her mouth to say...*what?*...and abruptly closed it again.

The right corner of Noah's mouth lifted and Morgan felt her irritation levels climb. 'What are you smirking at?' she demanded.

'You, of course.'

Of course.

'Well, stop it! Why?'

Noah lifted one shoulder and looked at her as he put the water bottle to his lips. Lucky water bottle... *Really, Morgan! Do try to be less pathetic, please.*

'You're sitting there thinking that politeness demands that you have to talk to me and the only thing you want to talk about is why I walked away so long ago.'

The ego of the man! The arrogant, condescending, annoying son-of-a... He was *so* right, damn him.

'I haven't thought of you once since you left,' she said, with a credible amount of ice in her voice.

'Liar,' Noah said softly, his eyes sparking with heat. 'You've *also* wondered what it would've been like...'

Also wondered? Did that mean that he had too? And why was she even having this conversation with him? In fact, why was he talking at all? The Noah she knew needed pliers and novocaine to pull words out of him.

'Well, I see that you've grown some social skills. Have you found that talking is, actually, quite helpful to get your point across?'

See—she could do sarcastic. And quite well. *Hah!*

'My partner nagged me to improve.'

His partner? Who was she? How long had they been together? Did they have children?

Noah laughed softly. 'You have the most expressive face in the world. Why don't you just ask?'

'Ask you what?' Morgan feigned supreme indifference. 'I have no idea what you mean.'

'Again...*liar*. When I say partner I mean Chris—my business partner.'

Single! Yay! Her girl-parts did a stupid happy dance and she mentally slapped them into submission because he hadn't really answered the question.

'And you?'

Morgan lifted her perfectly arched dark brown eyebrows at him. She knew that they were the perfect contrast to her blonde hair. And they made her eyes look greener than they actually were. 'That has nothing to do with you.'

Noah grinned and disturbed the million bats squatting in her stomach.

'You are such a duchess.'

Morgan bared her teeth at him. 'And don't you forget it. And, just to make it clear, I do not—*ever!*—want to discuss Cape Town.'

'It's a nice city.'

Morgan growled. 'What we *did* in Cape Town.' She pushed out the clarification between clenched teeth.

'*We* did? All *I* did was kiss you—you were the one who was naked and hoping to get lucky.'

She was going to kill him...slowly, with much pleasure.

Morgan ground her teeth together. How was this *not* discussing the issue? Did he not understand the concept of letting sleeping dogs lie? Obviously not.

Noah pushed his hair away from his face and rubbed his hand across his jaw. 'As much fun as it is, exchanging barbs with you, I do need to say something about Cape Town.'

Please don't. I've been humiliated enough.

Noah looked at her with serious eyes. 'I should've handled it—you—the situation—better, Morgan.' He held up a hand as her mouth opened and she abruptly shut it again. 'It took guts to do what you did and I was cruel. I'm sorry.'

Morgan realised that she was wearing her fish-face and snapped her teeth together. He was apologising? Seriously?

'So, that's all I have to say.'

Ah… It was more than enough and, quite frankly, she'd still prefer to pretend it had never happened. But she had to respect him for apologising, although she had played her own part in the train wreck that had been that night.

She rubbed her suddenly sweaty palms against her thighs. 'Okay, then. Wow. Um…thanks. I suppose I should apologise for hitting on you naked. I was rather…in your face.'

'A woman who looks like you should never apologise for being naked,' Noah said, humour sparking in his eyes.

It made her want to smile at him and she wasn't quite ready to do that. Nearly, but not quite yet.

'Can we…*ahem*…put it to bed?' he asked.

Morgan rolled her eyes at the very unsubtle pun.

Way past time to change the subject, Morgan thought. 'Mum said something about you being on your own? That you're not with CFT any more?'

Noah nodded. 'I have my own company doing pretty much the same thing CFT are doing. Except that we're branching out into security analysis; this is our first job for MI. I'm here to make recommendations about what systems should be put in place to secure the collection. That's the first step. Hopefully it'll lead to us installing those systems.'

'Are you good at it?'

'Very.'

'Okay, then.' Morgan twisted her ring around her finger and half shrugged. 'Today aside, I don't have much to do with the ball, but I would hate to see anything happen to the collection. It's fabulous; the gems are magnificent and the craftsmanship is superb.'

'Nothing to do with the ball? I think your mum has other ideas.' Noah finished his bottle of water, carefully replaced the cap and placed it on the table. 'If we get the job to install the systems then I will make damn sure that nothing happens to the collection. My business would be ruined if a diamond chip went missing, and that's not a risk I'm prepared to take.'

Morgan went cold at the thought of losing the collection. The value of the pieces meant nothing to her, but the fact that her family was the custodian of Elizabeth of Russia's diamond ring, a pearl won by an eighteenth-century Maharani wife, and the first diamond to come out of the first Moreau mine, meant a great deal. They were valuable, sure, but they were also historically important.

But if Noah was in charge of securing them then she knew that they would be fine. He exuded an air of capability and competence and, like all those years ago, when she'd felt secure enough to hand herself over to him, she felt confident about the collection's safety.

Noah was reliable and proficient.

Everything she wasn't—outside of her design studio. He was a living, breathing reminder of why she could never organise the ball. She would be stepping so far out of her comfort zone… A million things could go wrong and probably would and she'd be left holding the can. Nope, this was her mum's baby and would remain so.

Besides, she so didn't need the stress, the responsibility or the hassle of dealing with the sexy and not-so-silent-anymore Noah Fraser, with his sexy Scottish burr and sarcastic smile.

'Come on—time to go,' Noah said, standing up.

He watched as she uncrossed her legs and stood up. He looked her up and down and his eyes crinkled in amusement.

'Looking good, Duchess. Of course not as good as you looked back then—'

'I was nineteen,' Morgan protested, conscious that she'd picked up more than a pound since she'd been a perfect size four. 'Anyway, I'm that not much bigger.'

'You're not big at all, Duchess; you know you look great. My point was back then you were naked.' Noah placed a hand on her back and pushed her towards the door. 'Naked is always hard to beat.'

'Taxi, Miss Moreau?'

Morgan sent Noah a look in response to the doorman's question.

He shook his head slightly and jammed his hands in the pockets of his pants. 'No, thank you. It's a beautiful afternoon; we'll walk.'

'Enjoy the rest of your day, Miss Moreau. Sir...'

Noah fell into step with Morgan as she turned right and headed to the traffic lights to cross Park Avenue. It was moments like this when he was reminded just how famous the people he protected actually were. When the doormen and staff of one of the most famous hotels in the world recognised you and greeted you by name, as numerous people had Morgan inside the hotel, you had pull, clout—a presence.

Morgan, surprisingly, took it all in her stride. She'd greeted some of the staff by name, introduced herself to others. She didn't act like the snob he'd expected her to be.

'Amazing hotel. I've never been inside before,' he commented as they waited for the light to change so that they could cross the road.

A taxi driver directly in front of them leaned out of his window and gestured to the driver of a limousine to move and a transit van dodged in front of another cab, which resulted in a flurry of horns and shouted insults out of open windows.

New York traffic...crazy. And they drove on the wrong side of the road.

Morgan, adjusted the shoulder strap of her leather bag, looked back at the imposing entrance to the hotel and smiled. 'Isn't it amazing? I love it.'

'A couple of the staff nearly fell over to greet you. Must be crazy, being so well known.'

'Oh, I've been going there since I was a little girl; for tea, for dinner, for drinks—and of course we host the ball here every five years. It's a great place.'

'Great, yes. Safe? I'll be the judge of that.'

Morgan grinned. 'Oh, you and my Mum are going to get along just fine.'

It was a stunning spring afternoon for a walk back to the MI offices.

'Hey, Morgan. Over here!'

Noah turned around and a camera flash went off in his face. He cursed.

'Who's the dude, Morgan?'

A paparazzo, wearing an awful ball cap and a fifty-thousand-dollar camera, popped up. Seeing Morgan's thundercloud face, he lifted an eyebrow in her direction.

'This is why I hate going anywhere with you in New York,' Noah complained in his best petulant tone. 'Nobody ever pays any attention to *me*!'

Morgan looked startled for about two seconds before her poker face slid into place. 'Are you whining?' she demanded, not totally faking her surprise.

'I've been nominated for three BAFTAs *and* I've won a BSA but do I get the attention? No!'

Both Morgan and the pap looked puzzled. 'A BSA?' the pap asked, confused.

'British Soap Awards. And you call yourself a pap? Your UK counterparts would kick your ass!'

'Who are you again?'

It went against every cell in his body, but Noah forced himself to toss his head like a prima donna. 'Oh, that's just wonderful!' He looked at Morgan. 'I've wasted enough time—can we please go now?'

Morgan's lips twitched. 'Sure.'

Noah gripped Morgan's elbow and turned her away.

She sent him an assessing look from under her absurdly long lashes. 'Who *are* you again?'

Noah grinned. 'He's going to spend the next couple of hours combing through photos of Brit celebrities before he realises that he's been hosed.'

Morgan grinned. 'Excellent. Quick thinking, soldier. It won't stop him from printing the picture, but it did stop him from hassling me further.'

'Cretin.'

'Um…is there anyone back home that might get upset by seeing us together? If there is, you should give them a heads-up.'

Who would care if his photo appeared in a society column? It took a moment to board her train of thought. Ah…a wife, partner, girlfriend or significant other. He thought he saw curiosity in her eyes about whether he was involved with someone or not.

'I'll bear that in mind.'

Frustration flicked across her face at his reply. Yep, definitely interested—which was, in itself, interesting.

'Does that happen often? The cameras in your face?'

Morgan jabbed the 'walk' button to cross the road. 'All the time. It's deeply annoying and I wish they'd leave me alone.'

'Well, you *are* one of the world's wealthiest heiresses.'

Morgan's pulled a face as they crossed the famous street. 'Moreau International is wealthy—me, not so much. And I'm not that much of a social butterfly. Much to my mother's despair,' Morgan said quietly as she pulled oversized Audrey Hepburn sunglasses out of her black bag and slipped them on. 'Would you believe me if I told you that I'd rather pound a stake into my ear than attend a soirée or a cocktail evening?'

He wouldn't, actually. Look at her—she radiated confidence, class and poise. She was Morgan Moreau and her blood ran very blue. Unlike his, which was of the cheap Scottish whisky variety.

You're a long way from home, lad. Remember that.

'Then why do you do it?'

Morgan sent him a surprised look, opened her mouth to

reply and shut it again. She dodged around a group of teen-agers looking in a storefront window and looked resigned. 'So, what did you think of Sylvester Cadigan?' she asked a few moments later.

Change of subject, but he'd circle back round to her later. 'He seems competent. He wasn't happy that I demanded a complete and detailed dossier of the security arrangements they put in place for the last ball. He thought that I was questioning his professionalism.'

'Weren't you?' Morgan sent him a direct look with those bottle-green eyes.

'Sure I was. I don't trust anyone.' Especially when it was *his* rep on the line. 'I'll have a lot more questions for him to-morrow, after I've reviewed the dossier he's emailing me.'

'Do you need someone from Moreau to attend that meet-ing?' Morgan asked as they approached the gold and white façade of Moreau's Gems.

'No. We're going to investigate entrances and exits, look at the surveillance system. I think I can manage without someone holding my hand.'

'Good,' Morgan said, and gestured to the building in front of them. 'MI's flagship store, established in 1925.'

Noah looked at the façade of the jewellery store and swal-lowed down his impressed whistle. The very wide floor-to-ceiling window was lavishly decorated in a 1920s theme, Noah guessed. There were feather boas, deckchairs with tipped-over champagne bottles, strings of pearls hanging from or wrapped around silver ice buckets. Brooches pinned to berets left in sand, discarded chiffon dresses under a spec-tacular emerald and diamond necklace. Rings scattered in beach sand.

He hadn't passed the window when he'd arrived that morning, going directly to the separate doors that led up to the MI corporate offices. The window was fantastic and made him want to explore the store and see what other treasures were hidden within. And that, he supposed, was exactly the point.

'Amazing.'

'Riley's work,' Morgan replied proudly. 'She's utterly marvellous at what she does. She changes the display every month and she keeps it top secret. On the first of every month we all traipse down here, along with a horde of shoppers, to see what she's done. It's like Christmas every month.'

'She's very talented.'

'All the big stores keep trying to steal her away but she's loyal to us. Although she and James knock heads continuously. She demands carte blanche to do what she wants with the windows; James demands that she runs her designs past him first.' Morgan waved at a store employee through the glass. 'Having Riley and James in the same room is fabulous entertainment. They argue like mad. I can't wait to hear her ideas on themes for the ball.'

Oh, God, here comes the girly stuff. 'Themes? What's wrong with putting on some fancy duds and showing up?'

'*Pffft!* You sound just like my father. How would that be different from the other sixty balls happening in the city alone? We organise the *Moreau Ball,* not just *a ball.*'

Morgan turned away and headed to the MI entrance further down the street.

'How long will you be in New York for?' she asked, super-casually.

It was the first vaguely personal question she'd asked him and he wondered if he had imagined the flicker of attraction cross her face.

He was pretty sure *his* attraction had flashing neon bulbs and a loud hailer.

'If I get all the information I need I'll try and fly out tomorrow evening. I'll draw up my report, with recommendations and time-frames, then email it to you, James and your mother,' he said as they stepped up to the entrance of MI and the automatic doors swished open.

A guard gestured him to move away from Morgan; he stepped up to sign in at the security desk and to be patted down for the second time that day. Then he followed Morgan through the metal detectors and on to the bank of elevators.

'I'll arrange security clearance for you so you can swipe your way through,' Morgan said as they waited for a lift. 'Where are you staying tonight?'

The lift doors opened and they stepped inside. He could smell her scent, feel her heat, and their eyes collided in the floor-to-ceiling mirrors as he answered her question. 'In the MI company flat in the Lisbon Building, on West and Fifty-Seventh Street.'

'I know where it is. I live in the apartment above it. James, when he stays in town, is above me in the penthouse. My parents are in the family house in Englewood Cliffs.'

Noah shook his head. 'Never heard of it. Where is that?'

'Northern New Jersey, Long Island. About…hmm…ten miles from downtown Manhattan.' The tip of her pink tongue peeked out from between her luscious lips. It made him wonder what that mouth would feel like, how that tongue would taste. Still the same? Better?

'So, I'm single.'

Morgan looked confused. 'Okay. Thanks for sharing that.'

'You?'

Where was this going? 'Um…me too.'

Noah placed his shoulder against the mirror and couldn't believe what he was about to say next. His accent deepened as he spoke softly. 'Do you know something?'

'What?'

'MI have not, officially, signed any contract, so I'm technically not affiliated or contracted to MI yet. I don't think we're going to be working together, because you don't seem to have much inclination or willingness to organise this event…'

'Try *none*—and can you tell my mother that?' said Morgan, then frowned. 'And your point is…?'

'My point is that, technically, I can do this...' Noah stepped closer to her, placed his hands on her hips and dropped his head so that his mouth lined up with hers. 'I want to see if you taste the same.'

Morgan's eyes widened as her hands came up to rest on the lapels of his suit jacket. 'Uh...what are you doing?'

'Kissing you. Because we're both single, we're not linked by business, and because I want to,' Noah whispered against her lips.

They were as soft as they looked, as piquant as he remembered. They softened under his and he lifted his hand to push it under the weight of her hair, encircling her slender neck with his large, hard hand. Morgan whimpered and arched towards him, her hands snaking up his chest to link behind his neck. She stood up on her tiptoes and his tongue darted out to touch hers.

All sense of propriety and sensibility left him as he spun her around and pushed her up against the wall. His hand roamed the backs of her legs and under her butt cheeks as he lifted her hips into his erection, felt her breasts flatten against his chest. She was so hot, so feminine, and she was as into this kiss as he was.

All he could think was, where had he found the strength to walk away all those years ago? He wanted her—now— and considered pulling her to the floor...except that they were in a lift and the doors could open at any second...any freakin' second.

Noah pulled his hands off her butt and yanked his mouth off hers. He backed away—two steps, big deal—and tried to control his heaving breath. Morgan looked no better: shell shocked, kiss-bruised lips, strips of colour across her cheekbones. Anybody who saw them now would know exactly what they had been up to.

Morgan kept her eyes on his face and when the lift opened onto the executive floor, where they'd been earlier, she watched him get out. When Noah realised she wasn't following him he placed his hand on the door to keep it open and looked back at her.

'You aren't getting out here?'

'I'm going up to my studio. Top floor. Bye. And, Noah?'

'Yeah?'

'That was one helluva kiss.'

CHAPTER FOUR

MORGAN HAD DELIBERATELY not thought about his kiss all day. Well, she'd tried not to think of his kiss... Okay, truth: she hadn't thought of much besides his kiss!

To put it another way, she'd done little more than stare out of the window for the whole afternoon.

She was glad to be home, glad to be in her apartment where she could drop all manner of pretence and admit that Noah's lips on hers had rocked her to her core. She staggered over to her plump red and white striped couch, dropped her bag to the floor and sank down into its welcoming softness.

She'd kissed Noah Fraser.

Inside her body, every single cell she possessed was in revolt. A picture of the little molecules on a protest march flashed in her head...grumpy little cells each carrying placards with various sayings like: *Do Him!*, *We Want Orgasm Reform!*, or simply, *Sex! Now!*

She couldn't argue.

Her body craved Noah, and she wished she could use the excuse that she'd had none for a while...but she had, surprisingly, not so long ago. It hadn't been 'rock my world' sex, but it had been nice, pleasant, fulfilling and, best of all, very, very discreet.

With her high profile she valued discretion. She just hadn't realised that in that case *discreet* had been a synonym for married. She'd been surprised and shocked when—at the last minute, admittedly—she'd decided to attend a cocktail party she'd said she wouldn't be at. He'd been there with his very beautiful, very thin Venezuelan wife and they'd both known that her tipping a glass of red wine into his lap, accidentally on purpose, had been a poor substitute for her slapping him into next year.

Morgan placed her thumb on one eye and her index finger on the other and pushed.

She had kissed Noah Fraser. Again.

Actually, kissed was totally the wrong word… She'd inhaled him, Frenched him…devoured him. She could still feel his long fingers searing through her pants, the rasp of his two-day beard, the silkiness of his hair as she pulled it through her fingers.

He kissed liked a dream, like a man should kiss: with authority, skill, strength and tenderness. If he made love like he kissed… Morgan whimpered as she felt the pool of heat and lust drop to her womb. She was minutes off an orgasm and that was from just the memories of his kiss!

What if he touched her breasts, slid his fingers…? She didn't know if she was strong enough to survive the experience.

It took her a moment to realise that someone was pounding on her door and she wrinkled her nose. James frequently came by when he was in town and hung out, mostly to avoid their mother nagging him into attending an event. James was as allergic to the social swirl as she was… Was she a bad sister if she pretended not to be here?

She didn't want to talk to anybody. She just wanted to relive Noah's lips on hers, his scent in her nose, the hard muscles she'd felt in his shoulders.

Bang! Bang! Bang!

Bats…

'Who is it?' she demanded in a croaky voice as she pushed herself to her feet.

'Noah.'

The only person she wanted to see and the last person she'd expected. Morgan yanked the door open and there he stood, jacket and tieless, his fist about to connect with the door again.

Morgan put out one finger and pushed his clenched fist down. 'You pounded?'

Noah placed his hands on her hips and without a word pushed her backwards and kicked the door shut behind him.

'Oh, well, just come on in,' Morgan said, trying for sarcastic and hitting breathless.

Noah dropped his hands from her hips and slapped them on his. 'I've been thinking...'

'Did you hurt yourself?' Morgan asked sweetly.

He ignored her. 'On a scale of one to ten, what are the chances of you being in charge of this ball?'

'About...hmm...minus one thousand and fifty-two.'

'Thank God.'

'Why?'

'Because I don't sleep with my clients. Or my colleagues. Ever.'

'You nearly beat down my door to tell me that?'

'Try and keep up, Moreau. I don't sleep with clients.'

Morgan, starting to catch a clue, felt her heart-rate accelerate. 'And since I'm not going to be organising the ball I won't be your client,' she said slowly as she wrapped her head around the implications of those words.

'There you go.' Noah nodded 'I walked away years ago...'

'I know. I was there.'

That was a conversation for another day, and right now she didn't give a foo-foo. She wanted to know if he was here for the same reason she wanted him here. So that they could take that hot kiss they'd shared in the lift to its logical conclusion. And if he was toying with her again she'd have MI Security toss his gorgeous body off the roof.

Noah's eyes glinted blue fire. 'I don't want to spend the next eight years wondering...'

Morgan forced the lust away in order to think. It was hard, but she had to do it. 'You're leaving tomorrow to go back to London?'

'More than likely. There's nothing more I need to do here workwise...at this time.'

'So you are here for one night...one incredible, exceptional, crazy night.' she said, enunciating each word. 'Are we on the same page, here?'

Noah pushed a hand through his messy hair. She could tell it wasn't the first time he'd done that this evening. 'Yeah. Deal?'

Phew! She was going to get lucky! All her little cell protestors threw down their placards, lay down and assumed the 'do me' position. Morgan considered doing the same.

'What do you say, Morgan?'

Yes! Stop talking and take me now, yes! 'Okay, yes, that's a deal.' Morgan started to lift her shirt. She wanted to get naked—*now.*

'Stop. Don't,' Noah said, his voice low and urgent.

Morgan looked at him, fear and fury flashing in her eyes.

Noah took two steps to reach her and clasped her face in his hands. 'Relax, Morgan, I just want to undress you myself. Inch by gorgeous inch.'

'Oh.' Morgan's hands fell to her sides. 'Okay.' She tipped her head back and up, so that she could look into his eyes. 'You think I'm gorgeous?'

'Very—and stop fishing for compliments, Duchess. Try kissing me instead.'

The warmth in his eyes was at odds with his teasing words and Morgan felt her lips tip up in response.

Noah dropped a kiss on her nose before swooping down and covering her mouth with his, his tongue sliding against hers, long and smooth. 'You sure you want to do this, Morgan?' he muttered as his hand palmed her butt.

'Still sure.' Morgan angled her head away so that he could taste her neck, that sensitive spot just under her ear. His broad hand covered her breast and shivers skittered over her skin. Her fingers went to his shirt buttons and soon her hands were on warm male flesh, hot muscle and sexy skin. Her fingers danced over a very impressive six-pack and over the V of hip muscle that descended into his pants.

Noah groaned in the back of his throat as he slowly pulled her T-shirt up her torso, his eyes darkening at the white scraps of lace that covered her full breasts. He pulled her shirt up and over her head and dropped it to the floor, before running a finger along the edge of the lace. 'Pretty.'

Morgan sucked in her breath as his finger touched her hard nipple.

He hooked his hand under the lace and revealed her breast to his sizzling gaze. 'Very pretty indeed.'

His hot mouth covered her as he flipped open her bra and pulled it down her arms. Groaning, he banded his arms around her and, kissing her mouth, walked her backwards to the plump couch, lowering her to the striped fabric when the seat hit the back of her knees. Noah knelt down in front of her and picked up her booted foot, glowering at the knee-high laced boots.

Noah cursed. 'This is going to take far too long.'

'Not so much.' Morgan grinned, reached around to the back of her calf and pulled a zip down the boots. 'Hidden zip.'

'Brilliant.' Noah pulled her boots off impatiently, yanked her pants down her legs, and Morgan giggled when he tossed them over his shoulder. He sat back on his haunches, still dressed only in his suit pants, and looked at her, naked but for a little scrap of lace at the juncture of her thighs. She'd thought she would feel self-conscious, shy, uncomfortable, but how could she feel anything other than sexy and powerful when such a hard-bodied, lusciously masculine man looked at her with pure approval on his rugged face?

Then Morgan saw momentary hesitation in his face, knew that his big brain was trying to crash their party. She was *not*

going to be denied this again… If she had to tie him down—
ooh, that sounded like fun—she was going to have this man
on top of her, around her, inside her.

She leaned forward and placed her hands on his bare
shoulders. 'Stop thinking. I want this. So do you. Tomorrow is another day with another set of rules. Tonight there
is just us…no work, no history, no flaws. Just two people
who want each other. Okay?'

'Yeah.'

Noah nodded and Morgan released her tension in a long
sigh as one hand came up to cover her breast, his thumb idly
brushing her peaked nipple.

'I have a question,' Noah said reverentially, his eyes on
her panties.

Morgan wished he'd shut up and get on with what was
important—i.e. giving her a mind-blowing orgasm—but she
made herself speak. 'Okay…what?'

'Do you still have a Brazilian?'

'Well, soldier, why don't you take a peek?'

Bang! Bang! Bang!

Their heads flew up and turned in unison. Both looked
at the door in utter disbelief.

Noah, his hand in her panties, lifted his eyebrows. 'Expecting someone?'

'Uh—no.' And she wanted them to go away, while she
and Noah got back to what they were doing…which was
him doing her.

And doing her rather well.

Bang! Bang! Bang!

'Morgs, you've got thirty seconds, then I'm using my key.'

'James!' Morgan looked horrified as she pushed Noah
away. 'Clothes—where are my clothes?'

'Scattered,' Noah said as he stood up. 'Get dressed and
I'll delay him.'

'Open the door, Morgan!' James yelled. 'And who is
with you?'

'We're coming!' Morgan yelled back.

'Not in the way we'd hoped,' Noah stated as he reached for his shirt.

'Shut up!' Morgan growled, wiggling into her pants. 'Pass me my bra.'

Noah scooped up her bra, threw it towards her and tucked his shirt into his pants. When she was dressed, he gestured towards the kitchen.

'Got anything alcoholic?' he asked.

Morgan nodded towards an antique drinks cabinet in the corner and flipped open the bolt to her front door.

'James,' she drawled, 'have you ever heard of the concept of calling before you arrive? It's called etiquette. I'm sure Mum tried to teach us some.'

Morgan turned away and walked towards Noah who, being a good Scot, had found her expensive bottle of whisky and was pouring a healthy amount into three glasses.

'Morgan.'

Something in her brother's voice had all the hairs lifting on the back of her neck and arms. She turned around slowly and really looked at her brother. His face was bone-white and there were deep grooves in the lines running down next to his mouth. His eyes, green like hers, were flat and hard in his face.

'What's wrong?' she demanded. 'Is it Mum?'

James lifted up his hands. 'She's okay…really she is, Morgs, but something's happened.'

Morgan sensed Noah's approach and instinctively turned to look at him. He was rolling up the sleeves of his shirt and paused briefly, lifting an eyebrow in James's direction.

'What are you doing here anyway, Fraser?' James scowled.

Morgan figured that James really wouldn't want the answer to that question. Besides, he was a big boy—he could figure it out himself. Instead she gripped the back of one of the kitchen stools and tried to find her voice. 'Mum? What's happened, Jay?'

James gave Noah another tough look before running his hands over his face. 'Mum had an...incident earlier tonight.'

'Define "incident",' Noah said, and all traces of her earlier lover dissipated with those two words. He was in work mode, professional to the core. Serious, smart, and very, very dangerous.

'Jackson was walking Mum through the parking lot of Luigi's—she was meeting Dad for supper—when they were jumped by three guys.'

'Who is Jackson?' Noah grabbed a glass and handed it to Morgan. 'Drink.'

'My mum's long-time bodyguard and driver,' Morgan answered, grateful for something to do with her shaking hand.

Noah passed a whisky to James and gestured for him to carry on.

'Luckily Dad and Henry—Dad's bodyguard—were in the parking lot at the same time and saw what happened. Jackson and Henry reacted quickly—' James released a huff of frustration and sipped his whisky. 'The bodyguards got into it with the kidnappers while Dad picked Mum up— she'd been tossed to the ground in the fight—and bundled her into the car.'

'But not hurt, right?'

'Grazed chin and knees, sprained wrist,' James replied, the muscle in his jaw ticking.

'It's okay, Morgan.' Noah reached over and squeezed her shoulder. 'She's fine. What then?'

'Our guys—especially Henry—are pretty tough, and they managed to subdue two of them. The other got away.' James banged his glass onto the granite counter and splashed whisky. 'Before the police arrived they told them that they were part of a group who were looking to exact retribution for the fact that MI are in the process of reopening an emerald mine in a remote area of north-east Colombia.'

'Why don't they want it reopened?' Morgan asked.

'The mining, trucks and security will interfere with the local drug cartel's transport routes, and with increased population will make the inhabitants less...*reliant* on the generosity of the drug lords. I also suspect they are mining illegally as well,' James replied. 'They said that there are orders out to get MI out of the region.'

'Really blethered on, didn't they?' Noah said, his voice bland.

'Sang like canaries,' James replied. 'Probably because they had a knee in a kidney or a wrist about to be broken.' James folded his arms and rested his bottom against the counter in front of the coffee machine. 'The bottom line is that they want MI out of Colombia and they will do it by...'

Morgan saw his hesitation, the way he looked at her. 'By...?'

'By trying to kidnap someone else. You, me, other executives. I have told the executives in Colombia to be on high alert, and we're doubling their security—and the mine's. But you and I are definite targets. I want protection for you.'

Not again, Morgan thought. She hated having someone follow her around, monitoring her movements...constantly hovering.

'I've called CFT. They will have someone here in two hours. So if you could just stay put until they get here?'

'And Mum? How are we going protect her?' Morgan asked.

'Dad is taking her to the house in the Cayman Islands. You know how secure it is out there.'

'Good. That's good.'

James sent her a direct look. 'Any chance of you joining her there?'

Was he insane? She had jewellery commissions to complete and deliver and—damn it!—with her mother gone someone had to organise the ball. Her mum couldn't do that from the Cayman Islands or anywhere else. She needed to be here—in the city. So who was left to do it? *Me... Damn!*

'I'll take the protection, if you think I must, but I'm staying put.'

James blew air into his cheeks. 'CFT personal protection agents will be here soon. Will you accommodate them?'

What choice did she have? It was at times like these when the reality of how different her life was from that of a normal woman her age became very clear. This was when the fact that she was a Moreau—part of a prominent, hugely wealthy family whose business interests could upset people even a continent away—really smacked her in the face.

That wasn't normal. None of this was normal.

'That's not going to happen.'

Noah made sure that his voice was low, cool and utterly non-negotiable. In unison, James and Morgan turned to him, both pairs of bottle-green eyes surprised and suspicious.

James's eyes hardened a fraction of a second before Morgan's did. He could see that neither of them appreciated him jumping into the conversation but he didn't care. He just folded his arms across his chest and narrowed his own eyes.

'I'm not remotely interested in your opinion,' James told him. 'I'm making arrangements for my sister's protection.'

'So unmake them,' Noah suggested calmly. 'I will act as her personal protection detail.'

'What?'

The siblings' faces registered surprised confusion—and, really, could he blame them? They'd both forgotten that close body protection was what he did, was his business. And wasn't he here for the express purpose of getting his company more MI business? That whole world domination thing?

That was a good reason why he wanted to be the one to protect Morgan, but there were others. Since leaving the unit he'd done lots of close protection before moving into training the new officers. He knew how up close and personal bodyguards had to get to their principals, and there was no way that he was going to allow any CFT hound-dogs that close to Morgan. Fact: the only person that was getting into her personal space in the near future was him.

And, lastly, he wanted the best for Morgan. And he was it. There was a reason why Amanda had offered to double his already stratospheric salary if he stayed with CFT. He was that valuable, that good. Morgan deserved the best, and that was him.

Fact.

'I'm here. I'm already working for you.'

'I didn't realise that sleeping with my sister was part of your duties,' James said, in a very cool, very dangerous voice.

Noah didn't react. Mostly because he felt like punching James on his perfect nose… He didn't like being caught on the back foot, but he had to respect James for calling him on it. If he had a sister he'd do the same. 'Technically, I'm not employed by MI yet—'

'And the chances of you ever getting on the payroll are decreasing rapidly,' James stated.

Damage control, Noah thought, and fast. 'I'm good at what I do, Moreau, and what happened or didn't happen here earlier has nothing to do with that. Morgan and I are both consenting adults and we have an understanding.'

James looked at Morgan. 'Which is…?'

Noah remained silent. Hey, this was *her* brother—if she wanted to explain, she could.

'Well?'

'This has nothing to do with you, big bro,' Morgan stated, lifting her chin.

'You're my baby sister!'

'But I'm not a baby! I can have sex if I want!'

Both James and Noah winced. Noah scratched his forehead and was grateful that *his* brothers didn't require him to monitor *their* social life, because this was the social equivalent of a kick to the groin.

Time to end this conversation, he thought.

'Moving on,' he said briskly, 'and back to the subject at hand. Call Amanda Cope from CFT and ask her who her best bodyguard was—*ever*. I guarantee she'll say me. She hates me, but she's inherently honest. You want and need the best person out there guarding your sister. I'm it and I'm already in place.' It wouldn't hurt to sweeten the pot. 'I'll also give you a fifteen per cent discount on my personal protection fees because I'm doing an analysis on the security for your ball.'

'I don't want you as my bodyguard,' Morgan said.

'Tough,' Noah shot back.

James ignored her and held Noah's stare for thirty seconds before pulling his mobile out of his pocket and scrolling through his contacts. He was actually going to call Amanda! *This could go badly wrong,* Noah thought as James greeted her.

Morgan gripped his wrist and her nails dug into his skin. Even though they were sharp, he still felt heat and lust and attraction rocket up his arm. If he got this right, then acting as her bodyguard was going to be a casual stroll through hell….with a hard-on.

'Noah! Listen to me. I don't want this…*you*!' Morgan hissed.

Noah gently pulled her fingers off him and held her hand in his. 'Shh, I'm trying to listen.'

'I'm going to kill you,' Morgan threatened.

'Later…'

James was speaking. 'I don't need to know why he left, or what you think Auterlochie are doing wrong in the market place, Amanda; this has nothing to do with the rest of your guards or my personal security detail. It's one guy, looking after my sister. I just need to know whether he's good or not.'

When James's frown lifted from a trench to a furrow Noah knew that she had been her customary honest self.

'The best agent you ever had? Well, then…' James disconnected and slapped his mobile into the palm of his hand.

He glared at Noah. 'Fifteen per cent discount on both jobs because you started off by annoying me.'

Ouch.

'Deal,' Noah agreed.

'And keep your hands off my sister,' James growled.

'Basic bodyguarding,' Noah agreed, and he knew that James wasn't sure whether he was messing with him or not. James still looked like a thundercloud so he looked him in the eye. 'I will be completely professional when it comes to Morgan, James. You have my word.'

Besides, her safety depended on it... He couldn't look out for danger if he was eyeing her rack. Or her butt. Or imagining those legs around his hips...

And, although it was a lot less easy to admit, he was grateful for the order to keep his hands off Morgan. She was the type of woman he normally avoided. One of the few women who had caught his interest on more than a physical level. She intrigued him—mentally, emotionally. There was more to her than being the Moreau heiress, the reluctant NYC socialite. And that scared the hell out of him. Besides, he was consumed by his business. He didn't have the time or the energy to give to a woman.

James's shoulders dropped as the tension seeped out of him. Noah knew that James considered his and Morgan's relationship now to be defined, bound by the two contracts he would sign with MI. But to Noah it was written in blood—because he'd given James his word. No agreement written on paper trumped that.

Noah held out his hand and James reluctantly took it. 'Anything happens to Morgan you're a dead man,' James told him.

'Anything happens to Morgan I *will* be a dead man—because that's the only way they'll get to her.'

James's face lightened with appreciation and Noah thought that he might, *maybe*, be back on relatively solid ground with the brother and boss.

'Do either of you care what *I* want or think?' Morgan demanded, her hands on her hips.

Noah shook his head and looked at James. 'Uh…no.'

Noah ducked the glass that she sent flying towards his head and winced when the crystal shattered on the expensive tiles. Maybe he should curb the off-the-cuff honest answers. Good thing she had the aim of a one-eyed toddler or that might have hurt.

And, more importantly, it was a waste of a very fine dram.

CHAPTER FIVE

WASN'T THERE A song about yesterday and troubles seeming so far away? Morgan wondered as she stomped back into her bedroom, kicking her door closed behind her. Yesterday's biggest problems had been how to re-set Mrs Killain's fabulous teardrop diamond earrings into a more contemporary, cleaner setting, whether or not to attend the opening night of the Ballet Belle's new production, and who to take to Merri's wedding.

In one day she'd been slapped with an additional job, an old almost-lover, the attempted kidnapping of her mother, and a new bodyguard whom she wanted to jump.

Bats! On a freaking broomstick!

Right. First things first. Think it through... Her mum's almost-kidnapping. *No, don't think of the 'what ifs'. Push the emotion away...*

Her mum was only superficially hurt, and by now both her parents were in the family jet on their way to a safe place. The house in the Cayman Islands was a well-kept secret and James would have arranged for additional guards for them. Her parents were out of harm's way. That was good news.

Right: problem two. With her mum out of town, someone had to get cracking on organising the Moreau Charity Ball, and it looked as if she was now that someone. How was she going to manage to do that and keep her dyslexia under wraps? The last thing she wanted was to see pitying looks on the faces of Moreau staff…or from anyone else. Unfortunately a lot of people still equated dyslexia with stupidity, and she couldn't just go around announcing, *I'm dyslexic, but my IQ is one hundred and forty-eight.*

No, her dyslexia was *her* issue to deal with, and she didn't require sympathy, pity, or for anyone to make allowances for her. She'd just insist on short reports and plough through them at night…she'd make lists and check and double-check them.

Yay! What joy.

As for her almost-lover and new bodyguard…

She was intensely irritated with Noah on so many different levels that she wasn't sure which one she ranked highest. How dared he and James talk over her head and make arrangements for her safety as if she was a child? Okay, there was a crazy Colombian gang who wanted to use her as a bargaining chip, but Noah could have asked how she felt about him guarding her. She wasn't sure what her answer would have been if he had asked her… *No, I'd rather shag you instead*?

James would have had a coronary on the spot.

Noah irritation number two. How could he switch gears so easily and smoothly? Oh, she was royally ticked that one moment his hand had been tipping her into orgasm and the next he'd been all work—Mr I'll-Protect-Her-and-Give-You-a-Discount!

And on top of that there wasn't any chance of her getting lucky now; she knew that Noah took his duties seriously, and if he wouldn't sleep with her while she'd simply been organising the ball then there was an ice chip's chance in a fat-fryer that—having taken on the role as her bodyguard—he'd even consider picking up where they'd left off earlier.

And, really, did she want to get it on with a man who could flip it on and off with such ease? He had too much control and she too little…where he was concerned.

Well, no more. She was going to stop acting like a tart around him; she'd be cool and calm and collected.

Cool. Calm. Collected. Yep, she could do the three Cs!

'Sulking?' Noah asked from the doorway and she whirled around, her heart slamming against her ribcage. She had shut the door behind her, hadn't she? She was sure she had...

'Heard of knocking?' she demanded, hands on her hips.

Noah crossed one ankle over the other as his shoulder pressed into the doorframe. 'There's broken glass and whisky all over the floor and it's not in my job description to clean up because you lost your temper. Or are you too precious to use a dustpan and broom?'

'Bite me.'

Noah smiled. 'Can't. I promised your brother I wouldn't lay a hand—or lip—on you.'

Morgan felt the bubbles in her blood start to pop.

'You don't have to sound so pleased about it!' Morgan stormed to the doorway and brushed past him, the red mist of temper clouding her vision. What was it about this man that made her long for more? They didn't know each other really, but the fact that he could brush their heat off so easily made her want to throw more than a glass.

Maybe him. Off the twenty-first-floor balcony!

Noah reached out, snagged the waistband of her pants and pulled her to a stop. 'Cool your jets, Morgan, and take a breath.'

'Let. Me. Go,' Morgan muttered through clenched teeth.

'No,' Noah's said.

His fingers were warm against the bare skin of her lower back. She cursed the tremors of attraction that radiated up her spine.

Noah kept his fingers bunched in her pants and moved round so that he was standing, far too close, in front of her. 'Talk.'

More orders? 'Bite me,' she said again

'Stop being a duchess and talk to me. Why are you so annoyed that I am guarding you?'

Morgan folded her arms across her chest to form a barrier between their bodies and glared up at him. 'You didn't want to listen to me when I spoke earlier—why should I bother talking to you now?'

Noah winced. 'Okay, maybe we were a bit heavy-handed.'

'Maybe?'

'Don't push it,' Noah snapped back. 'I wanted to be the one to guard you and I was damned if you were going to talk James out of it.'

Morgan glared at him. 'Because I'm a way to get in with James for you to get more MI business.'

Noah's eyes darkened with fury. 'Stuff the MI business. I did it because no one will protect you as well as I will. Being kidnapped is not a walk down Madison Avenue, Duchess!'

'Uh...'

Noah shoved his hand into his hair and tugged. 'God, you live in this protected little world, kidnapping threats or not. You have no idea what happens to rich people who are 'napped. You want me to go into details?'

Morgan, her temper rapidly subsiding, shook her head.

'So sue me for wanting to keep you safe above wanting to have sex with you!' Noah roared, twin flags of temper staining his cheeks.

He stepped back from her and she could see that he was trying to control his temper. So he had one? Why did that reassure her rather than scare her?

Morgan tipped her head. 'You don't like losing control, do you?'

He lifted a finger and pointed it at her. 'You...you...nobody spikes my temper like you!'

'Ditto,' Morgan replied quietly as green eyes clashed with blue. After a tense, drawn-out silence, Morgan raised her shoulders and spoke again. 'Are you finished yelling at me?'

Noah released a long breath and slapped his hands across his chest. 'Maybe.'

'Okay, then.' Morgan pushed her hair back behind her ears. 'So, I'll go and clean up the broken glass.'

Noah nodded. 'I need to go downstairs for five minutes to pick up my bag and laptop.'

'Well, at least I have a spare bedroom this time.'

Noah rubbed his forehead. 'Does it have an inter-leading door that can stay open?'

Morgan shook her head. 'No.'

'Then we sleep with the doors open.'

'That's not necessary. We have two doormen, and this is one of the most secure buildings in the city.'

'The doors stay open.' Noah walked to the door and when he reached it turned to face her. 'I can't allow myself to be distracted by you, Morgan. Your safety depends on it. So help me out, okay? No propositions, no flirting, no walking around naked.'

There was that arrogance again, and she hated the fact that it turned her on. Determined to show him that he didn't affect her, in any way, she lifted her nose in the air. 'I'll try and restrain myself.'

'You do that, Duchess.'

Noah stood on the balcony in the bright sunshine and looked down into the leafy greenness of Central Park, idly noticing that the park was full of early-morning joggers, cyclists, walkers. Whoever would have thought that Noah Fraser, that angry boy from Glasgow, would be standing here looking at one of the best views in the city. Certainly not him. If he ignored the fact that Morgan was a kidnapping target and he couldn't touch her now, it was one of those stunning spring days.

Spoilt, unfortunately, by his father's voice whining in his ear...on and on and on.

Noah had been sixteen when he'd lost his mother and

taken over the care of his paralysed and violently angry father and his two brothers, six and four years old. And if Michael had been a mean bastard on two legs then he'd become even worse on none.

Noah had cooked, cleaned and cared for his siblings while Michael had cursed God and cursed them. By keeping Michael's attention directed on him, he'd managed to shield the kids from the worst of his verbal and—when he had the opportunity—physical abuse.

Noah had adored those little monsters, and it had nearly killed him when Social Services had moved them into the care of his aunt—his mother's sister. It had been the right thing for them—Michael could have scarred a psychopath—but he'd felt as if his heart had been torn out of his ribcage. Aunt Mary had offered to take him in too, but someone had had to look after Michael; his mam would have turned in her grave if he'd been left on his own.

'You might be poor, Noah, but poor men can act with honour too.'

'What is honour exactly, Mam?'

'It's taking responsibility and keeping your word. Seeking the truth and acting with integrity. Doing the right thing whether people are looking or not. Being better than your circumstances.'

Those words, part of a discussion they'd had a couple of months before her death, had defined the rest of his life.

It was because of those words that he'd endured three years of being belittled, insulted, punched when he was within range, before he'd cracked. It had been the most terrifying moment of his life when he'd come back to himself and realised he was holding...

Don't think about it. Don't remember. Put it back into the cage you keep it in.

He seldom relived the full memory of that horrible day, but every day he recalled how close he'd come to the edge after losing control. The consequences of which would have been far-reaching and…dismal. Catastrophic.

The very next day he'd joined the army—the best decision of his life. Yeah, it had been tough at first, but he'd got three square meals every day and, while he'd been shouted at all the time, he'd realised that it wasn't personal. He'd tolerated it at first and then he'd loved it; it had become, in a way, an inadequate substitution for the family he'd lost.

He'd moved around in the Forces, eventually ending up in the SAS.

Before leaving for Catterick, for his initial training, he'd arranged for a local care-giver to provide Michael with the help he needed: cooking, cleaning and, he'd hoped, occasional bathing. The cost of his care had come out of his meagre army salary, but it had been a small price to pay for his freedom.

He was still paying.

'Your brothers haven't called or visited for over six months.' Michael moaned.

He didn't blame them.

'Useless, both of them. Living with those Robinsons has made them soft… Mike is working as a nancy photographer and Hamish is no better. A bloody chef… Jaysus…and you paid for their education. Waste of money, I tell you. They'll never amount to anything.'

The fact that Mike was working on a respected national newspaper and Hamish was working in a Michelin-starred restaurant as a sous-chef had passed Michael by. With their crazy schedules the brothers didn't spend nearly enough time together, Noah thought. While they emailed and called regularly, they didn't meet often and he missed them.

He had to make more time for them…

'I said I wouldn't take your calls any more if you slag off Hamish and Mike, Michael. Don't do it again,' Noah warned.

He wished he could break the ties with this old man but he was his father. *Family.* Warped, possibly nuts…but you didn't just walk away from your responsibilities. You took what was tossed at you and you dealt with it. But, hell, hadn't he paid enough, done enough, sacrificed enough?

Michael did have one use, though: he was a reminder of how dangerous Noah could be if he lost control. Apart from Michael, the only person who'd managed to push his buttons, to get past the steel lid he kept on his emotions, was that blonde bombshell next door.

And that scared the bejesus out of him. Why her? He'd met a lot of women over the past fifteen years. He'd had successful girls, poor girls, crazy girls and, after he'd finished guarding them, a couple of famous girls.

None of them had made him think of *what ifs* or *maybes*, of moving below the surface stuff of good sex and a couple of laughs. No one except Morgan had ever tempted him to walk into the minefield that was a committed relationship. He'd grown up watching his mother trying to keep her head above water with his crazy, cruel father and he had no intention of being swept away by love and spending the rest of his life trying to get back to shore.

But the fact remained that nobody made him crazy like Morgan Moreau.

Morgan looked up as Noah entered the kitchen via the balcony door. He looked decisive, authoritative, commanding: a natural leader that others looked up to. Dark suit, a white shirt over that broad chest, sombre grey tie hanging loose down his shirt to be tied later.

He also looked freakin' hot!

A shoulder holster held what looked like a very nasty gun...*whoa!*

'When did you get a gun? And from whom?' Morgan demanded, wide eyes on its black matte handle-butt-thingy poking out from the holster.

'It was dropped off early this morning,' Noah replied, heading for the coffee machine and reaching for a cup from the shelf above it. 'Don't worry, I'm licensed to carry a concealed weapon.'

Morgan gripped the back of one of the kitchen counter stools. 'You didn't have one in Cape Town.'

Noah flipped her a look over his shoulder as he tossed sugar into his black coffee. 'Yeah, I did. You just never saw it. Ankle holster when I was wearing jeans. Tucked into the back of my shorts or in my rucksack when we were on the beach. You weren't considered too much of a target so we took the decision not to scare you.'

'Huh.' Morgan wrapped her hands around her now cold coffee cup. Had she been that oblivious? Sure, she'd been nineteen, and blinded by the mammoth crush she'd had on Noah. He could have had a third leg and she would have ignored that too…

So, had anything changed? Morgan wondered. Actually, yes. There was a difference between crushing on him and crushing on his body. This thing between them was purely, utterly, comprehensively physical. *That's my story and I'm sticking to it,* she thought.

'Have they heard anything else about the other kidnappers yet?' she asked. If she knew anything about Noah then she knew that he would be on top of the situation, demanding updates as any came in.

'It's only been twelve hours, Morgan. And they've probably gone underground. New York is a city of eight million people; it's easy to disappear. It'll take time, hard looking and luck to flush them out.'

Morgan sighed and rested her chin in the palm of her hand. 'So, I'm stuck with you for the foreseeable future?'

'Seems like it,' Noah replied equably.

Morgan fiddled with the flat gold chain that rested against her emerald silk top. She'd teamed the shirt with white skinny jeans and black wedges. A black fitted jacket and a scarf would take the outfit from casual to smart. She tapped her finger against her coffee cup and eyed him over the rim. Should she ask this? Hmm, probably not...

What the hey? she thought. *Let's see what he says.*

'So, who's Michael?'

Noah's blue eyes hardened. 'Where did you hear that name?'

'My bedroom window was open; you can hear pretty much everything anyone says out there.'

'I must remember that.' Noah sipped his coffee, leaning against the kitchen counter as he did so. Morgan twisted her lips in annoyance; Noah was an expert in ducking questions he didn't want to answer.

Except that her curiosity was revving in the red zone. There had been something in Noah's voice earlier that she'd never heard before. It had been a combination of resignation, weariness and resentment. A little younger and a lot sad. For a couple of minutes he hadn't been the hard-eyed, hard-assed man who radiated confidence and determination. He'd just sounded like a man with some baggage who desperately wanted to put it in storage.

'And who are Hamish and Mike? Come on—you can tell me...'

'So, what's your schedule like for today?' Noah asked, his expression warning her to back off. Way off.

She wanted to push, to dig a little deeper, a little harder, but it wasn't his grim mouth or ferocious expression that had her hesitating.

It was the misery she saw under the tough-guy expression in his eyes. He didn't intimidate her in the least, didn't scare her one iota, but that flash of desolation had her stopping in her tracks.

'Off-limits subject?'

'Very.'

'Okay.'

His jaw relaxed; his fingers loosened on his coffee cup. 'What are your plans for the day, the week?' he asked again.

'I still have to meet with Cadigan about the security for the hotel, but if you promise to stay in the Moreau building then I won't have to drag you to that.'

'Like you could drag me anywhere,' Morgan scoffed.

A smile touched Noah's lips. 'Want to test that theory?'

He didn't wait for her answer, obviously super-confident that he could and would. Well, he might be stronger than her but he had no idea exactly how stubborn she could be. She'd match her stubbornness against his strength any time.

'Where's your schedule?' he demanded again. 'Diary? Calendar? Or do you have an assistant to keep track of your social life?'

'None of the above. It's all in my head.' She had a diary which she never used, and she didn't need an assistant.

'Publicist? Stylist?'

'Now you're just mocking me.' Morgan sighed and placed her forearms on the table. 'Once a week I call Mum's publicist and find out what functions are on for the next week that I absolutely *have* to attend.'

'How do you know that you've been invited?' Noah asked, pulling out a chair from the table and sitting down. He reached for an apple and crunched into it.

'It sounds ridiculous, I know, but we—the Moreaus— are invited to everything. It's a big social coup to get us to a function…well, maybe not so much my mother; she's a lot more socially active than my dad, James and me.'

Noah looked at his apple, took another bite, chewed and swallowed. 'You guys seem really happy, close…together. A golden family.'

Morgan leaned back and crossed her legs. 'Every family has its own problems, whether they are rich or poor. James spends far too much time alone because he's one of the world's most eligible bachelors. He can't trust a thing that comes out of any girl's mouth because he's convinced that they look at him and see an unlimited credit card, entry into a high social circle and houses all over the world.'

'What should they see?'

A smart, successful man who was lonelier than he needed to be? She wished he'd find someone. She wanted him to be happy. He'd been fabulous growing up...had spent hours—days—years!—helping her to read and write. Holding her when she cried, picking a fight when she needed to work off her frustration. Her older brother, her protector, the best person in her life.

Morgan swallowed and shrugged.

'And you? What's so wrong in your life? You're rich, gorgeous, successful.'

Lonely, isolated, scared that someone will find out that I'm chronically dyslexic and will judge me for it. Terrified to step out of my comfort zone; scared to try and fail... So frightened of disappointing myself and others that I'd rather not try something than run the risk of failing...

Yeah, she was a poster child for a healthy and happy It Girl.

'I have...issues... Don't we all?' See—she could duck the very personal questions too! She twisted the oversized Rolex on her arm and carried on. 'As for my parents—my dad and my mum love each other to death but can't live together long term...'

'But they're trying to revitalise their marriage,' Noah protested. 'She's handing over control to James!'

'James, for all intents and purposes, has been running MI for the past two years. They both pretend that Mum still has her hand in, but in reality James calls the shots and she likes it that way.'

Morgan let out a sound that was half a snort and half a laugh.

'Scenes like yesterday's happen every so often—normally when my mum wants something and doesn't know how else to get it. She wants me involved in MI and she's determined to get me into the fold. Organising the ball is the first step. I guarantee that if I'd refused to do it—as I had intended to—

she would've been back in the city within a week, organising the ball, poking her nose into MI business and driving James crazy. She'd also have been telling me that my dad drove her nuts and there was a reason why they lived apart.'

Morgan scowled at her coffee cup. 'I love my mother dearly, but she's a force of nature and determined to get her own way. If she could find the kidnappers she'd probably say thank you to them for forcing her to leave the country, because now I *have* to organise this damn ball.'

'Harsh,' Noah said, but humour glinted in his eyes. 'Paranoid too. So what's the big deal about this ball? Suck it up and do it.'

Morgan glared at him. 'Easy for you to say. Anyway, back to the original subject…'

'Your social life…or lack of it.'

'Which is about to change because I'm expected to go out and about, promote the ball and get a buzz going. Got a tux?' Morgan demanded.

'Not here.'

'You're going to need one if you intend to accompany me to these functions.'

'And I do.'

'The biggest danger I face there is being bored to death, closely followed by the effects of a rogue margarita or a cheeky cosmopolitan.' Morgan pushed her cup away.

'Listen—and don't shoot the messenger—I need to go as your date,' Noah stated. He lifted a shoulder at the annoyed look on her face. 'Yes, I know what I said…we now have a completely professional relationship. But somehow, miraculously, the kidnapping attempt hasn't hit the papers and the MI PR person and the police want to keep it that way. James has a bodyguard occasionally but you don't. You having one now is going to raise questions that they'd prefer not to answer. So they want us to…*pretend*. James called me this morning and issued the directive.'

Morgan looked at him, caught completely off guard. 'What? You've got to be joking.'

'Trust me, I'd rather just be the bodyguard,' Noah muttered.

Morgan held up her hand. 'So, let me see if I've got this right. We were about to make love, because you weren't— quite—working for MI and I wasn't going to have anything to do with the ball. A one-night deal that worked for both of us which didn't happen because *you* volunteered your close protection services and told me that I am categorically off-limits. And now we have to pretend that we are lovers? Is this a sick joke?'

'Either that or someone has concocted a great way to torture us,' Noah agreed.

Morgan held her head between her hands and closed her eyes. 'This is going to drive me crazy.'

'We can share the padded cell,' Noah agreed.

'Any chance of you resigning?' Morgan lifted her head and looked at him, hope on her face.

'Sorry, Duchess. Not a chance. I'd rather go mad with you than go out of my mind worrying about you if I were off the job. Burying you would also suck.'

Ah, nuts… That was a hard point to argue.

CHAPTER SIX

IN HER STUDIO Morgan squinted at her computer screen and groaned audibly. She was stuck on the first page of the computerised file that detailed all the steps for organising the Moreau Charity Ball and she was already frustrated. Irritated. And, worse, shaking with fear in her designer shoes.

Date of event determined?
Liaise with banqueting manager at F-G.
Determine specific target audience for personal invites.
Objectives set in accordance to mission statement and vision of MI Foundation.
Complete risk assessment; not only to security of gemstone collection but also to brand and customer perception.

Dear Lord, she thought fifteen minutes later, couldn't they use plain English—and why was it so vague? Where was the 'how to do' part of the list? She hadn't even been aware that the MI Foundation *had* a mission statement, and she'd thought the vision was simple: raise and donate money.

Dammit, *this* was why she shouldn't be in charge of anything more complicated than *See Jane Run*.

Her mother had to be taking a new hormone pill to think

that she could organise the ball—never mind her crazy idea of joining MI as Brand and Image Director.

Morgan swallowed the tears that had gathered in the back of her throat. 'I am not stupid,' she whispered under her breath, glaring at the screen. 'I am not stupid. I am *not* stupid.'

Okay, then, why do I feel so stupid?

Morgan heard the rap on her door and looked up to see Noah through the glass window. She tapped the tip of one index finger with the other, indicating that he should use the finger scanner to enter. Two seconds later the door was opening and Noah, *sans* jacket and tie, entered her studio. She hastily slammed the lid of her laptop closed and inwardly cringed. What could be more mortifying than Noah finding out the scope of her learning problems? There wasn't a lot, she decided as he held the door open and looked at the finger scanner.

'Nifty. A retina scanner would be better, but the fingerprint scanner isn't bad.'

Morgan leaned back in her chair and crossed her legs. 'If the scanner worked then I presume that Security gave you everything you needed to negotiate your way through this super-secure building?'

'Yep.' Noah looked around her studio and she winced at the mess.

On the wooden benches across one wall sat her presses and pliers, mandrels and blocks. Hammers, files, more presses. The wall above it was covered in sketches, some finished, of ring and necklace designs, all of which held the name of the client scribbled across it and the price quoted.

She bit her lip and wondered what he'd think of her studio, with its plants and cosy seating, battered bench and industrial lighting. Yeah, it was eclectic and messy, colourful, but it worked for her. She could sit down at the bench and fall into a creative space that exhilarated her and made time fly. Sometimes the designs changed from the original sketch she'd been working to, but she'd yet to have a client complain of the changes made since they were all, invariably, better for it.

She sighed. Designing jewellery was probably the only aspect of her life that she felt completely confident about.

Noah walked over to the bench and squinted at her sketches. She saw his head pull back and presumed that he was reacting to the prices.

'Can I ask you something jewellery-related?'

Morgan's head shot up—not so much at the question but at the note of tension in his voice.

'Sure.' Oh, yeah, his body was coiled tight, and she narrowed her eyes as he pulled his wallet out from the back pocket of his black pants. He flipped it open, dug in a tight fold and pulled out a silver ring with a red stone. He tossed it to her and she snatched it out of the air.

'What's the stone?'

Before looking at the gem, Morgan looked at the setting. The band was old silver, a delicate swirl of filigree, feminine but with strong lines. Lovely, she thought. Really lovely. Whoever had made the ring was a superb craftsman, she decided as she picked up her loupe and walked over to the window. Holding the ring between two fingers, she lifted the loupe to her eye, angled the ring to the light and the breath caught in her throat. Red beryl, one of her favourite stones; very gorgeous and very rare.

'Bixbite or red beryl. Very rare. Very valuable.'

Noah walked over to her, stared down at the ring and frowned. 'Nah, can't be.'

Morgan arched an eyebrow at him. 'You a gemmologist now, soldier? Trust me on this: it's red beryl, my favourite stone…probably set around nineteen-twenty. It would've been mined from the Wah Wah mountain range in Utah.'

'Huh.'

Morgan frowned when Noah reached out, plucked the ring out of her grip with possessive fingers and put it back into his wallet. 'Where did you get it? And why can't it be valuable?' she asked.

Noah just shrugged and Morgan put her hand on his arm to keep him from turning away. 'Answering my question is my price for the valuation.'

'It was my mother's—passed down from my grand-mother. I was given it shortly after she died and I've kept it with me ever since. It would be my lucky charm if I believed in lucky charms,' Noah said, with the reluctance of a child facing a dentist's appointment. 'Her family wasn't...wealthy, so I'm surprised that they possessed something this valuable.'

Forget reluctance. Now he sounded as if he was having root canal without pain relief. Noah did *not* like talking about himself or his family. She wanted to ask how his mother had died—and when—but his expression was forbidding. She wasn't brave enough to go there.

'It's very lovely. And it either belongs on a finger or in a safe, soldier,' Morgan said. His expression begged her to change the subject so she relented. 'How did the meeting go with the Head of Security at the Forrester?'

Noah turned away and walked over to the window, look-ing down on the busy road beneath them. 'I have some con-cerns that he needs to address. I'll put them in a report and email it to you.'

Morgan wrinkled her nose. 'Can't you tell me instead?'

'What is it with you and your hatred of reading reports?' Noah asked, resting his butt on the window sill. Sunlight picked up deep golden-brown streaks in his hair and cre-ated a bit of an aura around his head. He looked like a rough, tough, gun-toting bad-ass angel.

Morgan clenched her thighs together and ignored the puls-ing down below. She really had to get her hormones under control. This was beyond ridiculous.

'Uh...reports. They are just a hassle to read.'

Noah's eyebrows pulled together. 'You don't like reading?'

'Not particularly.'

Noah crossed his legs at the ankles and folded his arms. 'So, what *do* you read? *Tatler* and *Heat*?'

And there he went, making assumptions. 'If I don't like going out in society why would I want to read about it? Actually, *snob*, my favourite authors are Jane Austen and Ernest Hemingway. Harper Lee, John Steinbeck—all the classics.'

'But you just said that you don't like to read.'

Yeah, but not that I don't love books. She did love books— devoured them by the bucket load. Except that along with the paperback she bought the audio book, so that she could read along. Truthfully, she frequently just opted to listen and not read.

Morgan flipped Noah a look and saw that he was looking very confused. Right, time to change the subject before he probed a little deeper. She wasn't ready—probably would never be—to tell him about her dyslexia. It wasn't something she believed he needed to know— now or ever.

'I have a list of this month's events that I need to attend,' Morgan said, picking up the piece of paper she'd printed earlier from the email she'd received from Helen. She walked over to Noah and watched as he speed-read the document. Lucky man.

'Ballet? *Uck.* A ball? Save me... But I can handle the art exhibition; I really like Davie's work.'

'You know Johnno's art?' Morgan asked, surprised.

Noah folded his arms and tipped his head. 'Now who's being a snob? I went to his exhibition in London. Fantastic.'

'Do you have any of his pieces?'

'Duchess, I could only afford to look—not buy.' Noah drawled. 'Maybe one day. Anyway, my partner can't find my tux in my flat. I think it's at the cleaners and has been for the last six months.'

'You left your tux at the cleaners for six months?'

'I've been in and out of the country and I forgot, okay? My tux wasn't high up on my list of priorities. So when do

I need a tux by…?' He looked at the piece of paper she'd handed him. 'Crap! Tonight?'

'Yep.' Morgan laughed at his look of horror.

'Jeez, give me some warning next time.' Noah grumbled.

'Hey, *I'm* the one who has to decide what to wear, do my hair, shoes, jewellery. Make-up. You just have to put on a tux. Big deal,' Morgan shot back. It took work to look like the Moreau heiress people expected to see. A designer dress, stunning salon hair, perfect make-up. The right jewels for the right dress.

'Yeah, but I have to get a tux and get into character…you know…work out how I'm going to pretend to have the hots for you. It's a difficult job, but someone has to do it.'

She was so distracted by the humour dancing in his eyes that it took a while for his words to make sense. When they did she blushed from head to toe and her fist rocketed into his bicep. It made all the impact of a single drop of rain falling in the desert.

'Jerk!'

'Was that supposed to be a punch?' Noah asked, and grinned as she shook her fingers out. '*Wuss.* So, are you going to stay here for the rest of the afternoon while I go and buy myself a tux? Can I trust you to do that?'

Morgan shoved out her lower lip. 'Maybe.'

Noah's face hardened and his mouth flattened. 'You leave this building without me and there will be hell to pay, *Duchess.*'

Morgan pulled in a huge breath. She didn't mind him calling her Duchess, but not in that cold, bossy voice. 'I'm not an idiot, *soldier.* I won't leave until you get back. And if you weren't being such a jerk I'd tell you that if you went across the road to that very famous store over there—' she looked past him and pointed her finger towards the renowned corner shop '—in the men's department there is a salesperson named Norman. In his sixties, bald. Tell him I sent you and he'll sort you out with what you need.'

Morgan was surprised when Noah leaned over and placed his cool lips, very briefly, on her temple. 'Thanks.'

Morgan watched him walk away, and he was at the door before she realised that kissing her was out of bounds too. 'Hey, no kissing!'

Noah tossed her a grin that had her blood pumping. 'Just practising for later. Do some work, Duchess, you have a ball to organise.'

Morgan wrinkled her nose. Sad, but true.

Being a bodyguard pretending to be her latest conquest sucked, Noah thought a couple of hours later in the ballroom of the Park Hyatt, half listening to Morgan as she talked 'ball' to a society matron with a pigeon-egg-sized diamond in her wrinkly cleavage. Doing it with a twitching groin made the situation a thousand times worse.

It was her dress, Noah decided, taking the smallest sip of the glass of whisky he'd been nursing for hours. Moss-green and strapless, it fell from her breasts and skimmed her hips. At first glance it almost seemed demure, slightly bohemian, off-beat. Then she moved and the long slit to one side exposed most of a slim thigh and his blood belted south. That thigh was smooth and silky, and even sexier because nothing covered it except perfect, perfect skin.

Funny and interesting… She was a killer combination. Bright as anything too. She picked up sarcasm, nuances, innuendo and irony, and he could read humour, annoyance and interest as the emotions flickered into her eyes. She'd been fêted all evening and he now realised what she'd meant when she'd said that the Moreaus were welcome everywhere. Conversation stopped when she joined a group, male tongues fell to the floor, women smiled and tried not to look jealous, and she was constantly and persistently asked about the ball.

'How do we get personally invited to the ball?'

'How much do you think we have to bid to secure a ticket?'

'Do you have a theme yet?'

'Do remind your mother that we served together on the blah-blah-blah committee and worked together on the meh-meh-meh project.'

Didn't these people have any pride?

But Morgan just smiled, changed the subject and moved on to another group if the person was too persistent.

'Don't you think so, Noah?' Morgan asked, and Noah sent her a blank look.

Morgan's lips lifted, and he knew by the gleam in her eye that she knew his thoughts were miles away.

'That this year's ball is going to be utterly amazing?' she clarified.

'Uh...yes...'

Wrinkly cleavage leaned across Morgan and showed him far more of what he didn't need to see. 'So, how long have you two been dating?' she demanded.

Oh... Noah looked at Morgan and waited for her to answer.

'We've known each other a long time, Vi,' Morgan said softly, her eyes on his mouth.

The twitch turned to an ache.

'Well, he's a lot better that a lot of those other creatures you've dated, Morgan.'

Morgan's lips lifted with amusement and she tipped her head. 'You don't think he looks too bodyguardish? All "don't mess with me or I'll wipe the floor with your face"?'

'Sitting right here,' Noah reminded them.

'Is that a bad thing?' Vi demanded. 'He *does* have very nice shoulders.'

'Mmm...and a nice butt.'

Noah glared at Morgan and lowered his voice. 'Morgan... enough.' As in *Behave yourself or I'm going to retaliate.*

He knew that she'd got the message because her eyes narrowed at his challenge. Noah looked up at the waiter who had placed the next course in front of her and saw the other plate he held—*his* plate!—wobble as his young knees buck-led under the force of that smile. He couldn't blame him, so he snatched at his plate before the mini-cheese platter ended up in his lap.

Morgan smiled at him before turning to another man on the table. Noah sneaked a look at his watch…it was after eleven already, and people were table-hopping or getting up to dance.

Maybe they could leave soon…

'Morgan, my honey, it's so nice to see you. We don't see enough of your pretty face at these events.'

Noah lifted his eyebrows at the plummy tones and looked at Morgan. The man had his eyes fixed on Morgan's chest and his manicured fingers rested on her shoulder. Noah, re-acting instinctively, slid his arm around the back of Morgan's chair, knocked his hand away and cupped her slim shoulder in his hand. Soft, silky…

Morgan turned slightly, leaned back towards him, and he caught a whiff of her hair: citrus and spice. Lust rock-eted to his groin.

'Morgan…' It was another voice demanding her attention.

Give the girl a break, Noah thought, turning to look up into the face of an elderly gentlemen who looked as if he could do with more than a couple of sessions in the gym and a year on a low-carb diet. Manners pulled them both to their feet and Noah watched as Morgan's knuckles were kissed in an old-fashioned gesture.

'It's so wonderful to have you here at the benefit, Mor-gan, and the room is abuzz with the news that you are taking over the reins of the charity ball from Hannah,' he gushed.

'Well, not quite, Alexander,' Morgan hedged. 'Mum is still in charge.'

'As you know, this ball aims to raise money for scholar-ships for deprived students in the poorer areas of our great city.'

Noah did an inner eye-roll at his pompous words, but Alexander wasn't quite done with the speechmaking.

'Our foundation was a recipient of a portion of the money raised from your ball five years ago, so I thought that you could do a short speech about the ball. In a couple of minutes? Wonderful.'

Smooth, Noah thought, he hadn't given her much chance to refuse.

'And who is your escort, Morgan?' Alexander held out a hand to Noah, which Noah shook. 'Alexander Morton—of Morton's International...banking, dear boy.'

Even when he'd *been* a boy he'd never been anyone's 'dear boy', Noah thought as he shook the soft, fishy hand and resisted the urge to wipe his own on his pants leg.

Morgan made a couple of standard responses to Alexander's queries after her family, but he could hear the tension in her voice, could see it in her suddenly tense jaw.

She was seriously and completely rattled. He wondered why.

Pretend they are naked, Morgan told herself as she gripped the podium and looked out over the expectant faces below. *No, don't think they are naked, you're feeling traumatised enough. They are cabbages...they are dolls...*

They were people waiting for her to fall flat on her face. She wasn't going to disappoint them...

Dear God, she thought, sucking in air, this was her worst nightmare. The room whirled and swirled. She couldn't find the words, didn't know what to say...what was she doing up here? She didn't—couldn't—do speeches, especially unprepared ones.

Her knuckles whitened and she gnawed on her lip as the murmurs from the restless crowd drifted up towards her.

Help. She pulled her tongue down from the top of her mouth and managed to find a few words. 'Um...good evening, ladies and gentlemen.'

Bats! What now? She couldn't think, couldn't find the words...*frozen, there* was the word. She was utterly iced up.

Then Morgan felt movement next to her and a large, familiar hand rested on hers and gently lifted her stiff fingers from the podium.

'Good evening, ladies and gentlemen, my name is James Moreau. Thank you for allowing Morgan and I a few minutes to tell you about the Moreau Charity Ball.'

James... She hadn't even known that he was at the ball tonight. Rescued again. Morgan briefly closed her eyes and felt the panic recede. *Thank you, my darling big brother.*

Morgan squeezed James's hand in gratitude and linked her fingers in his as she listened to his fluid off-the-cuff speech. He soon had his audience laughing and eating out of his hand...the smooth-talking devil.

'I owe you,' she said under cover of the applause. 'I was bulldozed up here.'

'Then bulldoze back, Morgs,' James retorted. 'What would you have done if I wasn't here?'

'I don't have a clue,' Morgan admitted as he led her back into the clapping fray. She tugged her hand out of James's and wiped her glistening forehead with the tips of her fingers. 'I need to visit the ladies' room.'

James gave her a critical look. 'You're as white as a sheet. You need lipstick and a shot of brandy.'

Morgan placed her hand on her sternum as her stomach churned. 'At the very, very least,' she agreed.

On the edge of the dance floor Morgan took the hand that Noah held out and stepped into his arms. He felt solid and strong...and best of all *real*. Just for a moment she wished she could place her head on his shoulder and rest awhile. This was why she hated the social swirl so much; the party-girl cloak she pulled on to get her through evenings like this weighed her down. She felt exhausted and such a fraud.

'So, what was that about?' Noah asked, his voice somewhere above her temple.

'What?' It was a stupid question because she immediately knew what he was referring to.

'James rushing to your rescue? I never imagined that you would be at a loss for words. You looked like your knees were knocking together.'

Why did he have to be so perceptive? James had assured her that they'd pulled it off, that most people had thought she was just waiting for him to join her at the podium, but if that was so then why had Noah noticed her nerves? And if he had noticed how scared she was, who else had? Oh, bats, did that mean that everyone was laughing behind her back? Sniggering?

She stepped back, lifted her hands and tossed her head. 'I want to go home now,' she told him, pleased that her voice sounded reasonably steady.

'Why?' Noah demanded.

Because I feel like a fool... 'I have a headache.'

'Not buying it, Duchess.'

Noah placed his hand on her hip, picked up her hand again and pushed her back into the dance. She followed his lead automatically and wished that the floor could swallow her whole. She felt hot with humiliation and cold when she thought about what was being said behind her back.

Morgan made herself meet his far too discerning eyes and didn't realise that her pulse was beating a hard rhythm in the base of her throat.

'Noah, I simply don't care whether you think I am talking rubbish or not. I'm done with this evening, I'm done talking and, frankly, I'm done with you too. I need some space and some time alone.' She shoved a hand into her hair. 'Can you, for once, just act like a bodyguard? Can you stop talking, keep your opinions to yourself and just leave me the hell alone?'

Noah's head jerked back and his implacable remote mask dropped into place. 'Certainly.'

He gestured to the edge of the floor and kept a respectful distance as they walked back to the table. His voice was devoid of emotion when he spoke again. 'If you'll give me a minute, I'll just organise the car.'

Morgan felt a wave of shame as she watched his broad back move away. She'd taken a hunk of his hide because she was feeling vulnerable and mortified. But mostly because she knew that he was strong enough, secure enough, to take it.

It was the perfect end to a long and terrible evening.

'Where's Noah?' Riley asked, dumping her files on the coffee table in Morgan's lounge. Sinking to the silk carpet, Riley took a grateful sip from the glass of white wine Morgan handed her.

After nearly a week of living together, in the non-biblical sense, Noah had finally realised that she was safe alone in the apartment by herself, and every day after work he left her to make use of the state-of-the-art gym and indoor swimming pool within the apartment block, Morgan explained.

'So, how does it feel to be living with a man?' Riley asked, kicking off her heels and crossing her legs.

Morgan sat down on the edge of the couch opposite her and half shrugged. 'Weird, actually.'

'And are you still in separate beds?'

Morgan glared at her. 'What do you think?'

'Judging by that killer look, I'd say your hormones are on a constant low simmer.'

'You should know,' Morgan replied.

As Riley was the only person outside of her family who knew about her dyslexia, Morgan was the only person who knew that Riley had fallen in love with James at first sight and had never quite managed to tumble out of it. She covered her feelings towards him by acting like a diva artist whenever he was around.

'He wants me to do an underwater theme for the windows next month,' Riley grumbled, reading her thoughts.

'Why?'

'Because he's just been scuba diving in Belize and was "blown away" by the coral reefs. I told him that I needed personal experience to do a theme like that.'

Knowing that would never have been the end of their conversation, Morgan tipped her head. 'And he said what in reply?'

'He used that super-sarcastic tone of his and said...' Riley tossed her bright red hair and lowered her voice. '"Then why don't I just take you with me next time?"'

'Jeez, I just wish you and James would get your stuff together, find a room, get it on and then get on with living happily ever after.'

'Like he's ever going to see me as anything other than your best friend.' Riley tapped her nail against her glass. 'Oh, wait—are you talking about us or about you and Noah?'

'Both of us. Although that won't happen to Noah and I.'

'Why not?'

'This thing between us is purely physical, Ri. We don't discuss anything personal.'

'Why not?' Riley repeated.

Morgan shrugged.

'Don't want to venture further down the rabbit hole?' Riley asked.

Morgan looked up at the ceiling.

'I think he might be the one guy who'd understand the dyslexia, Morgs.'

'I doubt it,' Morgan replied, leaning back and putting her feet up on the coffee table. 'He's a perfectionist: highly driven and ambitious. Besides, Noah and I...it would be just about sex—about this crazy chemical reaction we have to each other.'

'You like each other.'

'We don't *know* each other.' Morgan took a huge sip of

wine and rested the glass against her cheek. 'Anyway, I'm not looking for a relationship with Noah. Sex—yes...have you seen that body?'

'Shallow as a puddle.' Riley grinned before leaning back on her hands. 'To be honest, I think you don't tell the guys you date about the dyslexia because you hope they'll bail.'

'Oh, come on!'

'Oh, you *so* do. How many times have you met a nice guy? You date and then you sleep together. Things go really well until he starts picking up that things are a bit off. That you don't write down a message properly or you get the directions to a restaurant wrong. You don't explain and you retreat.'

'I don't do that,' she protested, even though she knew she did.

Riley gave her a hard look. 'Noah isn't like that, Morgan. He wouldn't hold the dyslexia against you.'

'Back away, Ri,' Morgan warned. 'Nobody understands until they have to live with me. You know what I'm like. Sometimes the reading is easy; other days I can barely read my own name. I would drive him crazy in six months. I'm inconsistent, and that's annoying and confusing. Some days I can take on the world; sometimes I can't even read simple instructions. I hate those black holes, and if *I* find them difficult to deal with how would my lover feel?'

'You should at least respect them enough to give them a chance to try.'

'I respect myself too much to be constantly putting my heart out there to possibly be broken,' Morgan retorted.

'Are you feeling comfortable in your little self-protected world?' Riley asked sweetly.

'Yes, thank you very much! The world expects something from "the Moreau heiress" and being chronically dyslexic isn't part of the package.'

Riley mimed playing the violin and Morgan threw a cushion at her head. Riley groaned as it hit her wine glass and wine splashed all over the table.

Noah walked in through the front door as the wine glass fractured and broke. He looked from Riley to the broken glass and back to the spilt wine before finally looking at Morgan. 'Duchess; are you throwing a temper tantrum because another of your subjects has disagreed with you?'

CHAPTER SEVEN

AFTER ORDERING PIZZA from their favourite pizzeria Morgan called James, checked that he was home and told him to come down and share their meal. He arrived with two bottles of her favourite wine: a Merlot from their winery in Stellenbosch.

'One for you and one for Riley, my two favourite wine-o-holics,' he said, depositing them on the kitchen counter. 'Hey, Ri.'

'James.'

James yanked open a drawer and pulled out a corkscrew. 'Started on the designs for my underwater window yet?'

'Yeah, I've scheduled it in for...*never*. Does that work for you?' Riley replied as she opened a cupboard door and took out four glasses.

'You *do* remember that I sign your paycheque, don't you?' James retorted.

'Then fire me; I'll pick up a job with Saks or Bergdorfs with one phone call. And they'll double my salary,' Riley replied in the same genial tone. 'Actually, why don't *you* double my salary and I'll consider staying?'

'Okay, I'll schedule that in for...*never*. Does that work for you?' James dumped some wine into her glass and handed it over. 'Cheers.'

'Bite me.' Riley took the glass and stomped over to the lounge, resuming her seat on the floor next to the coffee table.

Morgan rolled her eyes at Noah, who was sitting at the dining room table, his laptop in front of him, a glass of whisky at his elbow. He was dressed in battered faded jeans and a casual cotton shirt and his feet were bare. Sure, he was a sexy man, but he was also a man who didn't hold a grudge. They'd had a rocky day or two following her outburst at the ball and now they were back to being friends.

But it would be so much more fun if he was hanging around because he wasn't being paid to do so.

'Is anyone doing anything about finding those kidnappers?' she demanded, putting her hands on her hips and glaring at James.

'Only the NYPD, our own security and another private investigation firm I hired to find them. That not enough for you, Your Majesty?' James pushed a glass across the granite counter in her direction.

'Your Majesty? That's even better than Duchess!' Noah smirked.

'Call me that and you're dead,' Morgan warned him. 'Riley and I need to talk about themes for the ball,' she said, hastily changing the subject. 'Would you like to be part of that conversation?'

James and Noah exchanged identical horrified looks. 'Sports channel?'

'Hell, yeah!' Noah agreed, and followed James to the smaller second lounge. It held a large-screen TV and two comfortable couches.

He spoke over his shoulder to Morgan. 'Call me when the pizza arrives. I'll go down and get it. Do *not* leave the apartment.'

'Blah-blah-blah,' Morgan muttered in reply, and pulled her tongue at his back.

'I saw that!' Noah called, without turning around.

Morgan pulled her tongue again at his reply.

'I saw that too.'

Grrr.

* * *

'Treasure ship, masked ball, burlesque, the Russian Court, Vegas,' Morgan listed through mouthfuls of pizza. They were surrounded by files of fabric samples and Riley's rough sketches. Morgan was curled up into the corner of the couch, Riley was still in place on the floor, and James sat in the chair behind her, his long legs on either side of her slim frame. Noah sat in the other chair, a glass of gorgeous red wine on the table next to him.

It could be a group of friends in any other lounge in any other city in the world, just hanging out and eating excellent pizza. It was so normal, and he was still coming to terms with how normal the Moreau siblings could be. Yes, James ran a multi-billion-dollar corporation, and Morgan had an unlimited trust fund, but nobody, seeing them now, would guess that.

'I like the burlesque theme. Bold, opulent, sexy.' Morgan said dreamily. 'We could have various stages scattered throughout the ballroom with different acts to the same singer. Burlesque routines, circus acts, acrobatics...'

'Strippers?' James asked hopefully, and Noah smiled.

Morgan sent him a cold look. 'Would you like me to get disinherited? Or to be dead because our mother has killed me? Anyway, we could have models dressed in corsets and thigh-high stockings and masquerade masks, all wearing Moreau jewellery.'

Noah's head whipped up as her words made sense in his head. 'Not a chance,' Noah told her. 'No live models wearing any jewellery.'

'Why not?' Morgan demanded. 'It would be brilliant...'

'It would be stupid,' Noah replied. 'You're adding a human element that can be exploited; nobody but me and your curator gets access to those jewels.'

'But...' Morgan started to protest.

Noah stared her down. 'My reputation, my rules. Remember?'

'*Arrgh*. We'll discuss it another time,' Morgan said.

She was like a dog with a bone, Noah thought. Stubborn and wilful. Why did that turn him on? Then again, everything about her turned him on.

Riley leaned her head on James's knee and yawned. Noah noticed that James lifted his hand to touch her hair, thought about it and dropped it again. Oh, yeah, there was definitely something brewing with those two. Some day the lid on their self-control would pop and they'd find themselves in a heap of trouble.

Just like he would...

Living with Morgan was killing him. Not sleeping with Morgan made every day a torture. And he knew that she felt exactly the same way. He saw it in the way she looked at him; her eyes would deepen with passion and her breath would catch in her throat and he'd know...just know...that she had them naked and up against the wall. When...*if*...they finally got to do this, New York would experience a quake of significant proportions.

Unfortunately his problems with Morgan went a lot deeper than he'd ever thought possible. Right down to the core of who he was.

He'd never had such a physical reaction to anyone, *ever*. Why it had to be Morgan he had no idea. She could send him from nought to sixty in a heartbeat and have him laughing while she did it. And that was the reason why he had to keep his distance from her—physically, emotionally. He would never give anyone control over him.

She had the ability to make him lose it; definitely in bed, possibly emotionally and, most terrifying of all, in anger. She really knew how to push his buttons. What if they had a fight and he was pushed too far? What would he do? Who would he become? Would he revert to that angry feral boy who'd stood in that grotty kitchen and held a knife to his father's throat? The kid who had watched as droplets of blood beaded on that stubbled neck, enjoyed the sour smell of fear that permeated the air? The Noah who had seriously considered ending it all…the insults, the abuse, the weight of responsibility that had landed on his shoulders?

That person scared him: the uncontrolled, wild, crazy person he could be when he allowed emotion to rule. He was currently locked in a cage and sensible; controlled Noah kept guard over him. And sensible Noah could only do that if he stayed away from emotional complications. Like Morgan.

He couldn't afford to let Morgan in, to allow his guard down, to be the person he could be…

It wasn't going to happen with her or with anyone else.

'What do you think, Noah?' James asked him.

Noah pulled himself back to the conversation. What had they been talking about? Were they still discussing the theme of the ball?

'Burlesque sounds good,' he said lamely.

Morgan laughed as she tossed the crust of her slice of pizza into the empty box. 'Where did you go? We're talking about going home for the wedding. We're leaving in a fortnight.'

Noah sat up, ran a hand over his lower jaw and slapped his brain into gear. 'Back up. Going home? Where? What wedding? Why didn't you tell me about this?'

Morgan pouted. 'I'd hoped this would be over by then.'

'I asked you for a detailed schedule of everything you were committed to in the foreseeable future. Why wasn't this wedding on it?' Noah demanded. How was he supposed to protect her if she didn't keep him informed? Honestly, it was like dealing with an octopus with twenty tentacles.

Riley looked at James. 'I think this is our cue to leave so that they can fight without an audience.'

'I do not fight,' Noah growled. 'I negotiate.'

'No, he orders. He just tells me what to do and expects me to stand there and take it,' Morgan agreed, unfurling her long legs. She stood up, kissed Riley and then James on their cheeks as she said goodnight.

James hugged her, stood back and brushed her hair from her forehead. 'You're my sister, and I know you can be a pain in the butt. Don't make this harder for him than it has to be. Don't forget to tell him about Johnno's exhibition tomorrow night, and the Moreau Polo Cup Challenge on Saturday at Liberty Park. Then we go to the wedding in Stellenbosch in two weeks' time.'

'Got it.' Morgan cut Noah a glance, and when she spoke again her attitude was pure factitiousness. 'Noah, we have an art exhibition tomorrow night, a polo cup on Saturday and a wedding in Stellenbosch in two weeks' time. Put them on the schedule.'

Noah's face promised retaliation. *Bring it on, soldier.*

Noah bade Riley and James goodnight and waited until the door had closed behind them before turning back to Morgan. 'Stellenbosch, South Africa?'

'Yep,' Morgan answered flippantly.

He didn't respond—just waited for a further explanation for why she hadn't thought it was important to fill him in.

Morgan tapped her foot in irritation. 'The kidnappers are in New York. I'm going on the private jet to my home town, where I know everyone, to a wedding that has more security than the Pentagon.'

'Why?'

'Merri, my friend, is marrying into a very influential, very connected political family. Security will be tight.'

'And where will you be staying?'

'At Bon Chance—our house on the family farm. Vineyard.' Morgan picked up the empty pizza boxes and the bottle of wine. 'Grab the glasses, will you?'

'Good plan, since you might throw something when I tell you that I'm coming too.'

Morgan's shoulders stiffened at his sarcasm. 'I told you— it's not necessary. James and Riley will be staying in the house, as well as James's protection people, and the wedding will be secure. The kidnappers are here in New York!'

Noah walked over to the dishwasher, yanked it open and dumped the glasses inside. 'I'm going, Morgan. Until the threat to you is neutralised I'm sticking to you like a shadow. Now, I can either go as your date-cum-bodyguard or just as your bodyguard. I'm equally comfortable with either. Your choice.'

'That might be a bit awkward.'

Awkward... He didn't see why. Morgan turned away and Noah frowned. Strangely it took him a minute to make the connection. 'You've asked someone else to be your date?'

Morgan nodded. 'Yes. '

Noah managed to keep his face implacable but inside he fought the urge to punch his fist into that shiny, fancy fridge. 'Who is he?' he said through gritted teeth.

'A friend. An old friend.'

'That's not all of it,' Noah pushed.

Morgan whirled around. 'Do you want the details? Okay, then! He's an ex-boyfriend who I'm still fond of. He's also a friend of Merri's and we keep in touch. Satisfied?'

'Not by a long shot,' Noah snapped, forcing down the green tide of jealousy swelling up his throat. He made himself stop thinking about Morgan in someone else's arms— dancing, laughing, flirting with another man. This was business... What would he do if it was only business?

He breathed deeply and forced himself to think the problem through. 'If the security at the wedding is as good as you say it is, then I'll deliver you to the wedding and pick you up when you're done.'

Morgan's eyes sparked with anger. 'What if I want to sleep over?'

Was she trying to kill him? Seriously? 'That's not going to happen, Duchess, unless it's with me.'

'Big words from a man who won't even let himself touch me unless he's pretending to be my date!' Morgan hissed.

Give me strength, Noah prayed. 'I gave your brother my word.' He pushed the words out through gritted teeth.

'Well, there's no law that says I have to wait for you, soldier. So if I want to sleep with someone then I will.'

'You bloody well won't!' Noah gripped her arms with his
hands. His eyes glittered and he could feel his temper licking
the edges of his tongue. 'What would be the point, anyway?
You'd be imagining it was me the whole time.'

'You arrogant—' Morgan placed her hands on his chest
and shoved.

Annoyed beyond reason, he gripped her shoulders with
his big hands and fought the urge to shake her. Instead he
slammed his mouth onto hers and yanked her up against his
body. He placed one hand low on her back, fingers spread
out over her backside, and his other hand held her head in
place. Her made-for-sin mouth was hot below his.

Noah could feel her mentally fighting him, her mind curs-
ing him, even though he knew that her body wanted this as
much as he did. Pure orneryness kept her mouth clamped
shut, and her slim body was rigid with shock. Dropping his
hand from her head, he stroked her arm, urging her to relax,
and eventually both their tempers ebbed away under the sen-
sual heat they created.

He knew that Morgan was trying to fight the temptation
to wind her arms around his neck and fall into his body. It
seemed so long since he had touched her, and yet it was like
yesterday. She was toned, yet fragile, hot and sexy.

Noah concentrated on applying exactly the right amount
of pressure and kept his hands still. He kissed the corner of
her mouth and slowly worked his way inwards, nibbling and
caressing as he went along. His tongue flicked and retreated,
coaxed hers out to play. He sighed in triumph as she groaned
and opened her mouth to his. Instantly his tongue accepted
her invitation and curled around hers while he pulled her
close.

Unable to resist this a moment longer, Morgan threw her
arms around his neck and moulded her body against his.

Plunging her fingers in his hair, she wound a calf around his and pressed herself up against his hard frame.

Long, luscious, passion-soaked minutes later Noah knew that he'd reached the point of no return—that if he carried on for another minute he would be lost, doing exactly what he wouldn't allow himself to do. It took every ounce of his legendary self-control to wrench his mouth from hers, to step back, to meet her eyes.

He moved his hand so that he held her jaw, brushed his thumb over her full bottom lip.

Morgan spoke, frustration in her passion-smoked voice. 'You're really stopping?'

He nodded and jammed his hands into the pockets of his jeans so that he didn't reach for her again. 'Really am.'

He watched as Morgan's smoky eyes cleared and confusion replaced heat. 'I don't know why, or how, you can even *start* it. Especially knowing that you're not going to take it further.'

All he knew for sure was that he was a masochist, a glutton for punishment. He could try to explain—temper, jealousy, they were all factors—but his biggest motivator was that at that moment he hadn't been able *not* to kiss her.

Noah watched as the last spark of fight went out of Morgan. She took a step towards him, dropped her head and curled her fingers into his shirt.

'I hate this,' she said in a small voice.

And he hated the thought that he—this crazy situation between them—could make her sound so small, defeated.

He resisted the urge to pull her into his embrace, to soothe her. He didn't do touchy-feely so he just stood there, trying to ignore the surge of protectiveness that threatened to knock his feet from under him.

'Hate what?' he asked quietly.

'This…all of this. The bodyguarding. Being so attracted to you, not being able to touch you, to get it…*you*…out of my system.' Morgan rested her forehead in the middle of his chest. 'It's horrible... I don't like feeling this out of control.'

'I know.'

He had to touch her, so Noah rubbed his hand up and down her spine. It was killing him too. His hand moved up between her shoulder blades onto her neck and under her head. He pulled the hair at the back of her neck and gently tipped her head back.

'I gave my word...it's important to me that I keep it,' he said, looking down into her mesmerising eyes.

'I know. Dammit...I *respect* that. I just don't *like* it!'

Tell him something he didn't know. He didn't consider it a lazy day on the beach either.

Morgan stepped back, wrapped her arms around her waist and tipped her head to one side. 'I wish I could yell at you—scream. I want to act like a diva and fire you and stomp away and throw things.'

'You can if it makes you feel better,' Noah offered on a small smile. He had to hand it to the lass: he never knew what she was going to say or do next—she was *never* predictable.

'Consider yourself yelled at and fired,' Morgan said on a long, tired sigh. She looked at him. 'Any chance of you saving me from the loony bin and actually staying fired?'

Uh, no. That wasn't happening. A cold shower would happen, but him leaving...? 'Nope.'

'Didn't think so,' Morgan grumbled as she left the kitchen.

'This is it.'

Morgan looked out of the window of the cab and frowned when she didn't see the swish art gallery she'd expected to see. She looked across the road but there was nothing in the immediate vicinity except a closed dry cleaners and a rather grubby-looking diner. The other side of the street held a pawn shop and a strip club.

Where were they?

'Are you sure this is three-six-two?' Morgan asked.

Dark eyes glared at her from the front seat of the cab. 'You said six-three-two, lady. Three-six-two is uptown.'

Morgan closed her eyes at his harsh voice.

'Take it easy, buddy,' Noah said in a calm voice.

'She said six-three-two,' the cabbie insisted.

'You'll still get paid, so relax.' Noah laid a hand on her knee. 'Where's the invite, Morgan? Let's check the address.'

Morgan felt heat infuse her cheeks and rise up her neck and was grateful for the early evening shadows in the cab. She flipped open her clutch bag and pulled out the invitation. She glanced at the numbers and thrust the invitation towards the taxi driver.

'Six-three-two,' she muttered.

The driver glanced down at the invitation and shook his head in disgust. 'Jeez, lady, whassa matter wi' you? This says two-three-six!'

'Back off, man, she made a mistake,' Noah said in a hard, cold voice, and with a final huff the driver whirled around in his seat, slammed the car into gear and abruptly pulled off into the traffic.

Morgan licked her lips and waited for Noah's probing questions as they retraced their route. How was she going to talk her way out of this?

'Sorry.'

Noah shrugged and leaned back in his seat. 'You're tired...we both are. Mistakes are easy to make. Ignore him.'

Noah looked out of the window and Morgan glanced at his masculine profile. That was it? Where were the questions, the demands for an explanation, the mockery for making such a basic silly mistake? Why didn't he follow up on the cab driver's question, probe a little deeper?

Did he know and not care? Did he suspect and was distancing himself from the problem? Was he just simply not curious or, even scarier, didn't he give a hoot?

At the gallery a little while later, Morgan was still thinking of his non-reaction in the taxi and how she'd managed to dodge the explanation bullet. She stepped away from the group of people who were talking around her, looking past Johnno Davie at Noah, who was standing in front of one of Johnno's massive paintings. It was one of the few non-abstract paintings on display: a nude on a bed in a symphony of gold and cream, with hints of blush. It didn't need the tag *Sophie—Naked and Relaxed*; anyone with half a brain could tell exactly what Sophie had been up to before Johnno had decided to capture her on canvas.

Morgan wondered if Sophie knew that her...*ahem*...satisfaction was part of Johnno's latest collection.

Morgan lifted her glass of wine to her lips and watched Noah as he stared at the canvas. He was perfectly dressed for an art exhibition in NYC: dark jeans, a white button-down shirt and a black jacket.

Noah's immense self-control scared her—she admitted it. He'd been as swept away by their kiss last night as she had and yet he'd managed to pull back, to step away. She thought that she could be naked and he could be inside her, a fraction off orgasm, and if he decided to jam on the brakes he would. Oh, Morgan knew that he was self-motivated and determined, and that he kept his own counsel—that his natural way of interacting with people was to be brief and succinct, focusing on practicality above emotion—but even so sometimes she thought that there was another Noah trying to escape. A Noah who was a little more relaxed, a little impulsive—someone who was desperate to have a good time—but every time that Noah stepped over the line he got slapped back into his cage.

It was almost as if Noah was scared to let himself feel...

What had happened to him that had made him wary of... of...*himself*, really?

Morgan stared at his broad back as she walked over to him. She playfully nudged his shoulder with hers. 'I'm sorry about the confusion with the address earlier. I got the numbers mixed up.'

'Mmm…as I said, it happens.'

Morgan folded her arms across her raspberry-coloured poncho dress. It was a favourite of hers, with a one-shoulder neckline with a batwing sleeve. The dress fell to mid-thigh and she wore it with nude spiked heels and long, dangly ear-rings made from garnets.

'Listen, I need to say something. I'm sorry…about that kiss last night.' Noah held his hands in the pockets of his jeans and straightened his arms. 'I shouldn't have…'

'Here we go again… Noah, for goodness' sake, we are adults! We shared a kiss, and if you didn't have the control of a Tibetan monk we would've done much more.'

Noah glanced around as her voice lifted in frustration. '*Inside* voice, dammit!'

'What *is* the problem? And don't give me that garbage about not being professional and the promise you made to my brother.'

'Why don't you talk louder? I don't think the people at the far end of the gallery heard you,' Noah muttered as he gripped her arm and pulled her closer to the painting. 'And I *did* make a promise to your brother…'

Morgan turned her back to the room and looked at the painting. 'The old promise-to-my-brother excuse.' Morgan lifted up her arms and then fisted her hands. 'You know what…? Forget it! I've never chased after a man in my life and I am *not* starting with you!'

Noah muttered an expletive and raked his hand through his hair. 'Morgan…no, don't walk away.' He waited a beat before talking again. 'I've worked really hard to establish my business and, no matter how stupid you think it is, people *will* look to see how I conduct myself with you and they *will* judge that. I need to be seen to be professional and competent.'

Anyone would think she was asking him to do her in Cen-tral Park as Saturday afternoon entertainment. She saw him fiddle with his collar… He did that, she realised with a flash of insight, when he was feeling uncomfortable or when he was hedging. Or flat-out lying.

'That might be part of it but it's not the whole truth. The important truth.' Morgan looked him in the eye. When his eyes slid right she knew she had him and he knew that she had him. So he did what all men did when they were caught out: he changed the subject.

'Okay, say we have this hot fling. And afterwards, Duchess, what then?'

Morgan frowned and lowered the glass she'd raised to her lips. 'What do you mean?'

'We scratch this itch and then what happens? What are you expecting?'

Morgan took a sip of wine and considered his question. What did she expect? What *could* she expect?

What could she give?

After a moment's thought she came to the only logical, practical conclusion she could. 'I don't expect anything, Noah. You don't seem to be the type who needs or, frankly, wants a relationship, so if we did find ourselves in bed I'd expect nothing, because I know that you have nothing to give me.'

Besides, I'm too scared to take the chance of loving someone, being found unworthy, getting my teeth kicked in.

'You make me sound like a robot,' Noah muttered.

Morgan suspected that if he opened those cage doors he'd be anything but robotic—he'd be fearless and passionate and unstoppable. But right now he did have elements of the mechanical about him. Except when he was kissing her...

Morgan reached out and tapped his chest with one French manicured finger. 'You need to have some fun, Fraser. Lighten up.' Maybe they both did. 'The world won't fall on your head, you know.'

'You sound just like Chris. And my brothers.'

Whoa...stop the presses! Noah Fraser had volunteered some personal information! 'You have brothers?'

'Well, despite what you think, I wasn't cloned in a Petri dish,' Noah said, his tone grumpy.

'Younger? Older? Where are they? What do they do? Are they married?'

'Jeez, mention one little thing and I get a million questions.' Noah stopped a waiter, asked for a mineral water and rolled his eyes at her obviously curious face. 'Two much younger brothers, twenty-three and twenty-one. A sous chef at a London Michelin-starred restaurant and a freelance photographer who sells to several national newspapers. Neither are married and they both live in London. Satisfied?'

'Not nearly. Are they also buttoned-down, controlled and restrained?'

Noah took his mineral water from the tray presented to him. He looked past her shoulder to a place that was somewhere in the past. 'No, I stood as a shield so that they didn't turn out like me.'

And what on earth did he mean by *that*? Morgan opened her mouth to ask but he gestured to the painting and forced a small smile onto his face. 'It looks like a multiple to me.'

It took Morgan a minute to catch up, and when she did she cocked her head. 'Maybe it was a really good piece of chocolate.'

'Dream on,' Noah scoffed, before he fell serious. 'I have to admit I love this painting. I'd buy it in a heartbeat if I had enough cash floating around.'

Morgan leaned forward and peered at the tiny, tiny price in the corner of the tag. Holy bats…that was a lot of money—even for her. Morgan stepped back and looked at the painting again…she agreed with Noah. It was a sensational piece of art: fluid, sexy, happy. She could see it on the wall above her bed…

Sophie had had a really fine time, Morgan thought on a smile. But maybe it was time to give her a bit of privacy and get her out of the gallery.

'Let's go home,' Morgan said impulsively.

Noah looked at her, surprised. 'It's not even eight-thirty yet. And we were going to that cocktail party at the Hyatt.'

'I just want to go home, have a long bath and an early night. I want to drop the cloak. I need to be me tonight.'

'Sorry?'

Morgan waved his questions away. 'Ignore me. So, what do you think?'

'Hell, no, I *want* to stick around and make small talk with people I don't know.'

Morgan laughed at his sarcasm, handed her glass over to a passing waiter and inclined her head towards Johnno. 'I just need a quick word with the artist.'

'I'll be waiting at the door. Make it quick, Duchess.'

CHAPTER EIGHT

BACK IN MORGAN'S apartment, Noah glanced to the other side of the couch and smiled when he saw that Morgan had shuffled down, her head on a cushion, eyes closed and her sock-covered feet touching his thigh. Noah placed his beer on the side table and glanced at his watch; it was just past nine-thirty.

Standing up, he walked over to her and gently removed the earphones she'd plugged into her ears earlier. Her hand still loosely clutched her iPad and he pulled that away too. She liked listening to music while she read, she'd told him earlier, and wasn't that keen on TV, so he was welcome to watch what he liked.

Noah heard sound coming from the earphones and lifted one bud up to his ear. Instead of music, a low, melodious voice filled his ear. Frowning, he tapped the tablet and quickly realised that Morgan was listening to an audiobook, Ken Follet's *Pillars of the Earth*—a book he'd read years ago and thoroughly loved.

Noah had barely any time to react as Morgan launched up and tried to whip the tablet from his grasp. Her fingers skimmed the tablet as he moved it out of her reach.

'What the hell are you doing?' she demanded. 'Give it back!'

'Calm down, Duchess. Anyone would think you're hiding something here.' He grinned. 'Erotica? How to be an It Girl manuals?'

Morgan just glared at him, reared up and tried to take the device again.

'Oooh, temper. Now, I definitely know you're hiding something!'

'Stop being an ass! Give. It. Back!' Morgan shouted.

'Nah…I want to see what you're hiding. Bad music? Sappy movies? Your addiction to Angry Birds? Badly written cowboy books?'

'Noah!'

Noah tapped the menu and scrolled through her books. Frowning, he looked at the books on the device—there were many, and they covered a wide range of genres and subjects. But they were all audiobooks. He scrolled up, backwards, checked her files, and eventually realised that there wasn't a single e-book anywhere on the device.

'Only audiobooks, Morgs? Are you too lazy to read?'

He saw the colour seep from her face and her eyes fill with hurt. He frowned, knowing that he had misstepped badly, but he wasn't sure why his comment had had such an effect on her.

'Just give it back, Fraser,' Morgan said in a small voice.

Pride and defiance now flashed in her eyes, but underneath he could still sense her embarrassment and her vulnerability.

'My reading habits have nothing to do with you.'

'*Reports are a hassle to read.*'

'*Can you give me a verbal report instead?*'

He rubbed his jaw. Could it be…was it possible…that Morgan couldn't read? No, come on…*everyone* could read in this day and age, right? And she was so smart. There had to be another explanation.

Morgan sat back down on the couch and stared at the floor. Instinctively he balanced himself on his haunches and pushed her hair behind her ears, gently stroking the tender skin behind her ear.

'Do you have a problem with reading?'

She didn't reply and wouldn't meet his eyes. He hated to ask but he needed to know. 'Can you read…at all?'

Morgan jolted up and looked at him, her eyes wide and horrified. 'Of course I can read! Not well or fast, but I can read!' She stumbled to her feet, walked across the carpet and turned to look at him, her expression belligerent. 'Go on—say it. I dare you.'

'What?' Noah asked, genuinely confused.

Morgan placed a hand on her cocked hip and lifted her chin. 'I've heard them all, Noah—all the wisecracks, all the jokes. *She's got the looks and she's got money—what does she need a brain for? She's so thick that she'd get trapped on an escalator if the power went out. Quickest way to drown her? Put a mirror on the bottom of the pool—*'

'That's enough. Stop.' Noah held up his hand and kept his voice even. Who had said such brutal things about her? Whoever it was deserved a kick up the ass. It would be his pleasure to do it. 'Come and sit down, lass,' he said eventually, his voice gentle.

Noah waited until Morgan had perched on the edge of the couch, her bottom lip between her teeth. He resumed his position on his haunches in front of her.

'I'm not going to make fun of you, Morgan, but I do need to understand.' Noah rested his hand on her knee. 'Dyslexia?'

Morgan sighed. 'Chronic.' She glared at him again. 'But know this: I am *not* stupid, Noah. I have an exceedingly high IQ. I am *not* a dumb blonde.'

'Anyone with half a brain can see that.' Of course she wasn't stupid. She had the vocabulary of a Scrabble master and a brain that could tie him up in knots. 'You're probably one of the smartest women I know.' He ran a finger down her chest, skimming over her T-shirt between her breasts. 'This body is a work of art, but this—' he lifted his hand

and gently tapped her temple with his finger '—what's in here scares the daylights out of me.'

Morgan's eyes lightened in pleasure and a whole lot of relief. He smiled as a peachy blush spread over her cheekbones.

'It's just another part of you and you have absolutely nothing to be ashamed of. So, who was the loser?'

'The loser?'

'The guy who threw those comments at you. Name? Address? Name of the cemetery you want his dead body dumped at...'

Morgan's small smile disappeared quickly. She stared at her hands. 'First lover—a couple of months after you. I convinced myself that I loved him. He told me that I couldn't take a joke. He was verbally abusive but I gave him the ammunition to hurt me. Since then I've kept the dyslexia to myself.'

Noah uttered an obscenity and rubbed his hand over his face. 'Seriously, Morgs. Give me his name and I can cause him a world of pain.'

Morgan placed the tips of her fingers on his cheek. 'I appreciate the offer, but he's not worth the jail sentence.'

'You're no fun,' he complained mildly. She thought he was joking yet he'd happily use some of his nastiest unarmed combat skills on any man who so much as looked at Morgan the wrong way.

Noah sighed, looked at the shelves and shelves of books lining the walls surrounding them. How hard it must be to look at them but not be able to use them. 'So tell me about the paperbacks, Morgan.'

'I have a print copy for every audiobook I have. I used to try and read along, but the narrators read too fast so the words swim and dance and I get a cracking headache by page five.'

Noah unfurled his long length and sat down on the couch next to her. 'You don't need to keep it a secret, Morgan.'

Morgan dipped her head so her forehead touched his collarbone. 'Yeah, I kind of do.' She snuggled closer to him and his arm went around her slim back as he leant back against the couch. 'I'm not just a little dyslexic, Noah, I'm really bad. And some days I'm terrible.'

'Is that why you were so reluctant to organise the ball?'

'Yeah. It's too important for me to fail at it…and I don't want to disappoint my mum. It's hard, trying to live up to the Moreau name. The family are all terribly well educated— they all have two degrees; my dad has three—and I scraped through college by the skin of my teeth, taking twice the amount of time anyone else did.'

'You just told me that you are not stupid,' Noah pointed out. 'Surely they know that too? And as educated people don't you think that they admire you for trying something outside of your comfort zone? I know I do, and I only have one degree.'

'They keep telling me that. Maybe I'm just scared of disappointing myself.' Morgan tipped her head back to look at him. 'What do you have a degree in?'

'Business and history,' he admitted reluctantly. 'Love history. It's still my favourite subject.'

Morgan sighed happily. 'Then I must show you some of the old diaries from the first Moreau prospectors—the brothers who discovered the mines. They were wacky and colourful and quite unethical.'

'I'd love to read them.' Noah gently pulled her ponytail. 'You look exhausted, Duchess. Why don't you go to bed?'

'I'm tired, but I probably won't sleep,' Morgan admitted. 'My brain is whirling.'

'You need something to de-stress you.'

He stood up, scanned the bookshelves and found what he was looking for. Yanking the book from the shelf, he sat down again, stretched out his legs and tucked Morgan back into his side.

'If I remember correctly, you were just about to start chapter six.'

Morgan's eyes were as big as saucers. 'You're going to read to me?'

Her eyes filled with emotion and Noah winced. Oh, jeez, maybe he'd insulted her by offering to read to her. Maybe she hadn't heard a thing he'd said earlier about how smart he thought she was…

'I'm sorry. Look, it's not because I don't think you're… Bad idea, huh?'

Morgan's fingers on his lips dried up his words. 'No, it's probably the sweetest thing any man has ever done for me.'

Noah grimaced. 'Sweet, huh?'

'Yeah—very, very sweet.'

Noah pulled another face. 'Yuck, that's not how any ex-Special Forces soldier would like to hear himself described. Now, will you please shut up? I'm trying to read here…'

Noah handed Morgan a glass of champagne and, from behind his dark sunglasses, cast a look down her long, long legs. Every other woman at the Moreau Polo Cup Challenge was dressed to the nines, but Morgan, in tailored white shorts that ended at mid-thigh, and a white and green gypsy top revealing her shoulders and messy hair, looked every cent of the millions of dollars she was supposed to be worth.

Earlier, just because he was curious, he'd timed her to see how long she took to get ready. Ten minutes. He'd known women who took ten minutes to put on mascara. He really, really liked the fact that she didn't fuss.

And that she still managed to look super-hot.

'Do you ride?' Morgan nodded to the field and the charging, sweaty thoroughbred horses.

Noah snorted. 'Not many stables where I grew up.'

'Where *did* you grow up, Noah?' Morgan asked.

Well, he'd cracked the door open… Noah sighed, thought about ducking her question, remembered that she'd shared her biggest secret with him and told himself not to be a jerk. 'I grew up in Glasgow, in a bad part of town.'

Morgan kept her eyes on the field. 'Did you have a tough childhood?'

'Yeah.'

And that was all he was prepared to say. Besides, it was all such a long time ago. He was with a gorgeous girl at a fancy event and he didn't want those memories to corrode his enjoyment of this stunning spring day.

'So, tell me about your date for the wedding,' he said casually.

Noah frowned as a tall, slim Spaniard in a white polo shirt and jodhpurs streaked with dirt leaned over the fence, placed his hands on Morgan's shoulders, kissed her on both cheeks and then lightly on the mouth. Morgan laughed, patted his cheek, and conversed with him in passable Spanish. Their conversation ended with another flurry of cheek-kisses and, *dammit*, another brush of her mouth.

Noah resisted the urge to reach for his gun.

'Friend of yours?' Noah asked, unaware of the bite in his voice.

'Juan Carlos. Playboy. Polo player. He taught me to tango,' Morgan said in a dreamy voice.

'That had better be all he taught you,' Noah said in a low mutter.

Morgan's mouth twitched. 'A *duchess* never tells. Andrew—how *are* you?'

Kiss, kiss...flirt, flirt...

Noah looked at his water and wished he could ask for a whisky as she dived into conversation with yet another polo player who'd ambled up to greet her. She would drive any sane man to drink, Noah decided as a bead of sweat ran down his spine.

He wanted to remove his navy linen jacket but he wouldn't. He didn't want to raise questions about why he was wearing a sidearm to one of the most elite social events in the city. He was on constant alert at functions like these;

there was no security, people came and went, and anything could happen.

Unfortunately no one was close to finding the kidnappers and the tensions at the mine remained unresolved; in fact they had just got worse, and they'd all been warned to be on high alert.

James had flown out to Colombia to try and resolve the dispute, and a posse of CFT personnel were guarding his back. That was why James wasn't at the Polo Challenge and why Morgan would be handing out the prizes to the polo players—and no doubt kissing eight or more fit, rich, polo-playing numbskulls.

Oh, joy of joys.

Polo Boy number two walked away and Morgan pushed her glasses up into her hair and fanned her programme close to her face. 'What were we talking about?'

'Your date for the wedding.'

He caught the tiny wince. 'Oh…him.'

'Yeah, *him*. Want to come clean, Morgs?' Noah asked, a smile hiking up the corner of his lips.

Morgan placed her champagne glass on a tall table and sighed. 'I lied. I was trying to wind you up—'

'You succeeded,' Noah mumbled, thinking that it was the thought of her sleeping with someone else that had ignited his temper and led to the urge to kiss her, brand her, possess her. 'So, he's fictional?'

Morgan scuffed the grass with the tip of one of her apple-green wedges. 'Mmm.'

Noah slowly pushed his shades up into his hair and looked down into her face, idly thinking that he loved the handful of freckles on her nose that make-up never quite seemed to cover. 'Do you lie often?'

'No. Only when I'm pushed beyond reason.'

'I'm very reasonable.' Noah protested.

'Pfft.' Morgan rolled her eyes.

Noah rested his forearms on the fence. 'I've been thinking about something you said the other night at the art exhibition.'

'What did I say?'

'You said something about the cloak you'd like to drop… what did you mean by that?'

Morgan took a little while to answer. When she did her voice was softer, vulnerable. 'Don't we all have cloaks or armour that we drag on to protect us from the circumstances we find ourselves in? Something we do, or say, a way that we act to get us through whatever it is making us feel uncomfortable? A cloak that covers all our insecurities, the real us that we don't want people to see?'

Noah gave her words some thought. 'Your flirty, charming party-girl persona…that's your cloak? The bright, bubbly, charming flirt? The real you is quieter, more introspective… dreamier.'

Morgan cocked her thumb and extended her index finger. 'There you go. And you only know that because we've been living in each other's pockets. And your implacable and remote face that discourages all conversation is yours. Your can't-touch-me mask is supposed to discourage anyone from wanting to dig deeper, to get to know you a bit better.'

Noah couldn't help wincing. He did do that—did keep everyone at an emotional distance.

He rubbed his hand across his face. 'You've come closer than anyone—ever.' He caught the flash of fear in her eyes, saw her take the tiniest step backwards. 'And that makes you uncomfortable,' he added.

'Wary.' Morgan looked out at the busy field. 'We can hurt each other… No, let me rephrase that. You can hurt me…if we ever change from friends to lovers.'

'*If* we change—and I'll try not to, Morgan—you have to know that I wouldn't be able to promise you for ever. All I can say is that I would be monogamous, that I'd treat you well as long as it lasted—be it a week or months. But at some point our paths would split and I'd be back in London, doing what I do.'

'I know.'

'If you want more from me than a fun time in bed then maybe we should just quit while we're ahead. Stay as *Duchess* and *Soldier*.' Noah folded his arms and hoped she couldn't see how much he hoped that she didn't choose option B. Because that would, well...*suck*. 'So, what's it to be?'

Morgan played with the emerald and diamond studs in her ears. 'I'm probably going to regret this, but we do have unfinished business between us.' She sent him a coy look and the humour was back in her eyes. 'By the way, are you into threesomes?'

If he'd had anything in his mouth he would have sprayed her, or choked. As it was, he felt he had to pick his jaw up from the floor. 'What the...? Who? What? Are you being serious?'

'Well, by the time this situation is resolved my friend Sophie from the gallery will be sharing my bedroom. I thought I should warn you.'

Noah felt his heart slow down to a gallop as her words started to make sense. 'Morgan, you nearly gave me a heart attack! You bought Johnno Davie's painting?'

'I did.' Morgan smiled. 'It'll be delivered when the exhibition is over.'

They turned as someone called her name.

'Ooh, I'm being summoned. I need to go and hand out the prizes and flirt with the players.'

Noah couldn't help the possessive hand he put on her back, the growl in his voice. 'Keep it to a minimum, sweetheart. Remember that I'm armed and dangerous. I'd hate to have to shoot one of them.'

Morgan touched her lips to his cheek and whispered in his ear. 'Just to be clear, soldier, Sophie is the closest you are ever going to get to a threesome that involves me.'

He could live with that. Heck, he was happy fantasising about a 'onesome' with her.

A few days later Noah heard the lobby phone chime and got up from the dining table where he had been working on staff scheduling—his normal Auterlochie work hadn't stopped, so he worked from Morgan's dining room table or the MI conference room. He picked up the phone.

'Hey, Patrick.'

He'd become good friends with the doormen—both ex-cops, with excellent service records—and Patrick's voice boomed in his ear.

'I have Miss Riley here, plus two guys carrying mannequins and stuff. Can I send them up?'

'What? Hold on, let me take a look.' Noah walked backed to his laptop and pulled up the live feed from the lobby. Patching into the apartment building's security feed had been his first task when he'd moved into the apartment weeks ago. True enough, there was Riley, chatting to two young guys holding two life-size mannequins.

Why was Riley bringing mannequins up to the apartment? He wasn't sure he wanted to know.

He went back to the phone and thought for a minute. The situation in Colombia had descended into near anarchy and threats were flying. Hannah and Jedd were still not allowed to leave their house in the Cayman Islands. He'd spent twenty minutes on the phone with James earlier that day and they'd agreed that Morgan should curtail her social obligations. So now he had to try and keep her in the apartment as much as possible...which would be a butt-pain, because resisting the urge to haul her off to bed was now on a par with him splitting the atom.

'Put Riley, the mannequins and the bags into the lifts and send the men home. I'll help her unload on this side,' Noah told Patrick, and went back to his laptop.

When the doors had closed on Riley and her plastic companions, he called to Morgan.

'Hey, Riley will be here in twenty seconds with some life-size dolls. Why?'

'Yay!' Morgan said, coming from the bedroom and towel-drying her wet hair. She draped her towel over the back of the couch and Noah fought the urge to ask her to put it back in the bathroom. He was obsessively neat, courtesy of the army, and she was a slob. Her untidiness drove him nuts.

Noah opened the front door, and walked over to the lift. As the doors opened he grabbed one mannequin and tucked it under his arm. 'Friends of yours, Ri?'

'Ha-ha.'

Riley handed him a duffel bag and he walked back to the apartment and dumped them in the hallway. He went back for the second dummy and Riley followed him, carrying the second smaller bag.

He watched, amused, as Morgan and Riley sat the mannequins—expensive ones, with arm and leg joints—on the colourful couches. Morgan squealed and immediately reached for the duffel bags. Thinking that they probably needed alcohol for whatever they were up to, he went into the kitchen and opened a bottle of wine. When he returned with two glasses in hand his eyes widened at the rainbow-hued lingerie now scattered over the coffee table. No, not lingerie...sexy-as-sin burlesque costumes. Beaded and decorated corsets with fluffy skirts and feathers. And there were some without skirts, skimpy, with oversized clips to attach to stockings.

His mind instinctively imagined Morgan in one of those outfits and he cursed when his pants stirred. High heels, stockings... He thought of the survival courses he'd taken in the SAS. Nothing sexy about those...

Thoughts of sex bolted away and his heart ran cold as Morgan picked up a duffel bag and a treasure trove of jewellery rained down on the table. Emeralds, rubies, diamonds, gold...so much gold. Pearls, sapphires... If Morgan had liber-

ated the MI jewellery collection from the walk-in safe on the
fourth floor—and he knew she had access to do that—he was
going to freakin' kill her. Slowly, and with much pleasure.

'Oh, my, look at his face.' Morgan chuckled as she held
Riley's arm and doubled over with mirth. 'Quick, grab your
mobile and snap a pic. We'll call it *Nervous Noah*.'

'In a moment you are going to be *Mortuary Morgan*,'
Noah replied as he approached them. He handed over the
wine and picked up a necklace with a canary-egg-size diamond hanging off a gold clasp. He examined the stone,
didn't see the deep sparkle and reflections a diamond that
size should have and his blood pressure dropped. 'Paste. You
nearly gave me a heart attack!'

Morgan grinned. 'They are all paste, and it's fantastic
that we have them to play with.'

Noah held up his hand. 'I think *I* need wine for this…hold
on.' He went back to the kitchen, brought another glass and
the bottle back and perched on the arm of the chair. 'Now,
what are you doing, exactly?'

Morgan crossed her legs Indian-style and with her wet
hair and make-up-free face she looked a teenager. Like she
had when she was nineteen, when she'd stolen his breath
from his lungs. Nothing much had changed there, Noah
thought.

'Okay, so you said that we can't have live models showing off the collection…'

'Categorically not,' Noah said.

'So, Riley and I want to place mannequins on round
plinths throughout the ballroom, each of them in a gold burlesque birdcage *à la Moulin Rouge*. We'll put them in pro-
vocative poses—on swings, bending over, et cetera. The
mannequins will all be dressed in burlesque costumes—
sexy corsets and stockings, high heels and masks.' Morgan
picked up a handful of lace and stockings. 'The great thing
is that we have paste copies of all the jewellery collection

and Riley has the mannequins, so we can experiment before we make a final decision.'

'Why?' Noah asked.

Morgan, who was examining a pearl necklace, frowned up at him. 'Why what?'

'Why do you have paste copies of the jewellery collection?' Noah asked patiently.

'Oh...a Great-Something Moreau needed to raise some cash to buy another mine and he handed over the collection as collateral. He didn't want it known that he was cash-strapped, so before he did that he had paste copies made of the jewellery. He got the jewels back but ever since, whenever the family acquired a new piece, a copy was made. Riley and I played with these as kids.'

'Huh. So they are exact replicas?'

'Absolutely.' Riley draped a long string of pearls around her neck. 'So what do you think of our birdcage idea, Noah? Can the real jewels be secured?'

Noah thought for a minute. 'I want an area between the guests and the cages, about a foot and a half, where we can put a pressure plate so that if anyone steps up to a mannequin it'll trigger a silent alarm.'

Morgan looked at Riley. 'We can do that.'

'I want in on the design of the birdcages. I want to put laser beams between the rods, so that if anyone breaks the beam it'll trigger an alarm.'

Morgan lifted a bustier of white silk embossed with silver beads and waved his security issues away in order to play with the colourful garments and the fake bling.

'Okay... Look at this one, Ri! Such a gorgeous red, with black inserts, and the feathers make a teeny-tiny skirt. If we teamed it with those striped thigh-highs...dynamite! Let's dress a mannequin in an outfit, choose the corresponding jewellery and mask, photograph it and do the next one. And where on earth did you find all these outfits?'

'A burlesque show that lasted six weeks on Broadway.

Apparently the costumes were fabby, the performers not so good.'

Noah put his wine down, stood up and picked up a mannequin, looking it over.

'What on earth are you doing, Noah?' Morgan asked.

'Seeing where we can place a motion sensor so if the jewels are moved once they've been put in place it will trigger—'

'A silent alarm.' Morgan and Riley chorused.

'Smartasses.' Noah dropped the mannequin and thought that he badly needed some testosterone before he started to grow breasts. 'I'm going to watch some manly sports on ESPN. Have fun playing with your grown-up Barbies, girls.'

Noah's hand drifted over Morgan's hair as he passed her. He wasn't sure if she noticed because she was frantically scrabbling through the piles of multi-coloured, beaded and luscious garments to look for...who knew what?

Concentrating on sport was a nightmare when he couldn't stop imagining Morgan in a tiny black and red corset sparkling with diamond-like beads, black striped thigh-high stockings, red 'screw me' heels and an elaborate Mardi Gras mask...straddling his hips, his hands on the smooth, warm, bare flesh above those heart attack-inducing stockings...

He dropped his head back against the arm of the couch and adjusted his jeans. Could a man die from lack of sex and frustration? He was convinced that it was a distinct possibility.

CHAPTER NINE

MORGAN KNOCKED ONCE on the conference door and popped her head in. Noah, on a video conference, flicked a glance at her, smiled, and looked back at his screen.

'I sent off the quote for that corporate security analysis in Hungary, Chris. I think we might—'

Morgan leaned her shoulder into the doorframe and waited for him to finish his conversation. Look at him—so sexy with his tousled hair and wire-rimmed reading glasses. Morgan felt the usual rush of lust, quickly followed by the warm and fuzzies. She suspected if they ever got to have sex he'd be an amazing lover: sweet and tender, hot and fast, slow but hot… She suspected that, like the many facets of his personality, the variations to his lovemaking would be endless. But right now she loved talking to him over the first cup of coffee in the morning, over a glass of wine at night, arguing about the fact that she was the untidiest person he'd ever met. She couldn't imagine him not being in her life and knew, with or without sex, that she could, if she wasn't very, very careful, fall chaotically, crazily in love with him.

She couldn't, shouldn't…wouldn't. Some day soon the situation with the Colombian mine would be sorted out and he'd go back to London, to his life and business there.

'Hey, what's up?' Noah asked, pulling his glasses off his face and resting his forearms on the table. A cup of cold coffee, his mobile and his wallet were placed in a neat row on the other side of his laptop and his sidearm was snug against his shoulder.

Morgan placed her hands behind her back. 'It must be really difficult, trying to run your business from here, Noah.'

Noah looked around. 'It's not so bad. I'm plugged into the server at work—it's practically the same as if I was working in my office and Chris in his. The only difference is arguing face to face instead of over Skype.'

'Well, I'm still sorry if guarding me is an inconvenience.'

'Better than the alternative of you being kidnapped. Or dead.' Noah placed his arms behind his head. 'How was your day? Still battling with the Barnado piece? Has she settled on a design yet?'

She was currently dealing with an ultra-picky client with the concentration span of a cricket. 'Nope. I've been wading through cost projections for the ball and my eyes are crossing.'

'Need some help?' Noah asked.

He asked it in the same voice he used when he wanted to know whether she wanted coffee. As if she was so very normal…and to Noah she was. Her dyslexia was just another part of her—like her untidiness or her freckles.

'Morgs, do you need help?'

Noah repeating his question pulled her back.

'I'll make time if you need me to.'

'No, I'm good. I heard from James; we'll be flying out at five tomorrow afternoon and we'll be in Cape Town mid Friday morning. I told Merri about you. She said that it's a garden wedding and one more person won't make a difference, so she's insisting that you attend with me.'

Noah raked his hand through his hair. 'If the security seems okay then I'm quite happy to leave you there, Morgan. I really don't feel like attending another stuffy function, talking to people I have nothing in common with.'

Morgan walked over to him, laid a hand on his arm and felt his warm skin beneath her fingers. He'd rolled up the sleeves on his casual duck egg blue button-down shirt and she could feel the raised veins in his arms. 'It won't be like that, I promise. Merri is a hoot—stunningly beautiful, but utterly laid back. And the rest of my good, solidly normal friends will be there... Ellie, Jess, Clem and their men. You'll like them.'

'Jeez, Morgan, I don't know.'

'Please, Noah?'

'Does anyone ever say no to you when you flutter your eyelashes and do your Puss-in-Boots look?'

Morgan's lips twitched at the corners. 'Not often, no.'

'Didn't think so. Do I have to wear the tux again?'

'It's a garden wedding. No tux needed.'

'Finally a sensible bride.' Noah glanced at his watch. 'Are you ready to go home?'

Morgan shook her head to clear it. 'Actually, I wanted to tell you that I need to go into Moreau's Gems to see a customer. He's demanding a second opinion on a valuation Carl has given him and insists on getting one from a Moreau. Idiot. He made a scene earlier, and Carl made an arrangement for me to meet him after-hours—which is now.'

Noah frowned. 'Is that normal? Meeting clients after-hours?'

Morgan shrugged. 'Yeah, we meet with clients at the time that suits them, not us. Anyway, he's there now and waiting for us.'

'Security?'

'They aren't allowed to leave until Carl does,' Morgan said, cocking her head at them. 'It's a client, Noah, and it happens all the time. Fifteen minutes, in and out, and then we can order Thai for supper.'

Morgan saw the look he sent to his screen and the frustration that flashed in his eyes. 'I can ask one of the security officers from the lobby to see me there and back if you're busy. Fifteen minutes, tops.'

Noah seemed to be considering the option for a minute,

but he eventually stood up and pulled on his jacket. 'Nope. Let me just send an email delaying my next conference call and I'll come down with you.'

He bent over the screen and his hands flew over the keyboard. He hit 'enter' and picked up his mobile and wallet. Then his eyes met hers and her heart spluttered, misfired and coughed to life again.

Morgan held her breath as his strong hands encircled her jaw and throat and watched wide-eyed as he tipped his head and his lips hovered just above hers. She saw something in his eyes that she hadn't noticed before: something soft, almost tender. Morgan gripped his wrists with her hands and kept her eyes locked on his, waiting for him to swoop down and claim her lips in a kiss that she knew would blow her socks off.

She wanted to sink slowly into the hot whirlpool of his mouth. He would be more delicious than she remembered, far tastier than her imagination suggested. Noah caressed the side of her neck and she inhaled the intoxicating scent of his skin. If she moved a fraction closer she would feel the thrust of her breasts against his chest...their skin would only be separated by his shirt and her silk T-shirt.

Worse than the thumping lust that pooled between her legs, the rapid beat of her heart, was the thought that she was one step closer to losing her heart. It was slipping further away from her and she knew that if she allowed it to fall out of her hand it would be his for ever.

Noah stepped back, but his big hand still grasped the side of her neck and his thumb touched her jaw and tipped her head up.

He muttered an obscenity and her eyes widened.

'One of these days—hours—minutes—I'm not going to be able to step away from you.' Noah moved back and gestured towards the door. 'Let's get this done. I've still got work to do tonight.'

So did she—really important work, Morgan thought, troubled.

Like figuring out how to ensure she didn't fall in love with him.

Morgan had gone somewhere in her head, Noah thought as they hit the pavement outside MI headquarters and moved into the busy end-of-day crowds, and he had no idea where. He'd almost kissed her and then she'd got this weird look on her face and wondered off to a place where he couldn't reach her.

Maybe she was thinking about the design she was battling with, or the ball; he knew how much she had on her plate at the moment and was surprised at how well she was coping. The dyslexia popped up now and again, but he knew that it was nothing that she couldn't handle. It got worse if she rushed or was stressed, and he'd worked out that if he distracted her she frequently relaxed and could then read whatever she'd been stuck on before. He was also beginning to believe that her dyslexia was directly related to her confidence and her happiness; if she was relaxed she had far fewer problems than she did if she was stressed.

He knew that sex would be a brilliant distraction... *Promise to James, promise to James.*

The Moreau's Gems door was locked so Noah knocked. Morgan shook her head at him and pressed a discreet button on the side of the door. He heard a click and frowned when the door popped open.

'There are cameras inside Carl's office; they can see who is at the door,' Morgan said, grinning at his obvious paranoia.

'Where's the guard?' Noah asked as he pushed Morgan inside.

'Probably making coffee. I don't know, Noah! Jeez!' Morgan said. 'Come on, Carl will be in his office.'

Noah made sure the door was locked behind him and looked around. His Spidey Sense was going nutso. It was the same feeling he'd had numerous times in the army, when he'd known things were going to go to hell in a handbasket.

Cold shivers ran down his spine and he instinctively *knew* that he'd just walked them into a heap of trouble. He placed a protective arm around Morgan's waist and pretended to nuzzle her ear.

'If I call you Duchess, you drop like a stone to the floor,' he said, in a low voice that only she could hear.

Morgan—funny girl—rolled her eyes at him as they approached the main counter holding a precious display of some of the world's best gems set in amazing designs. He withdrew his gun and Morgan's eyes widened.

'What the heck are you doing? Put that away. It'll go off and you'll hurt someone!'

Seriously? He was a highly trained operative and if he made it 'go off' then he'd damn well be intending to hurt someone. *Honestly—civilians!*

He made the mistake of sending her a pointed look and out of the corner of his eye saw movement. The next minute a boot connected with his wrist and his gun went flying. Where had he come from? he thought as he dodged a knife-swipe at his belly. He heard Morgan's whimper, ignored it, saw an opening and ploughed his fist into a throat. His attacker crumpled.

Then all hell broke loose.

Noah yelled at Morgan to move and shoved her out of the way as he bulleted over a counter and slammed into the space behind—where a suited thug waited for the opportunity to gut him like a fish. Noah waited for the attack, grabbed the arm attached to the knife, broke his ulna and launched his elbow into a temple. Out of the corner of his eye he saw another shadow and his foot flew out and connected with the chin of another knife-wielding lout who'd come to his friend's aid. It just glanced off a granite face and he came at him again.

The fight was a blur of motion…kick, punch, kick from

both of them. Noah knew that he couldn't worry or even think about Morgan just yet—not while he had to contend with this better-trained and skilled attacker. Noah bounced on his toes, waited for his opening and hooked a fist into his sternum, following up with a well-placed kick to his groin. Just because he was angry, he picked the guy up and tossed him into a counter. Glass and jewellery flew out of the case.

Whoops!

'Stop.'

The voice came from behind him and every muscle in Noah's body contracted. He wiped his bleeding mouth with his hand before slowly turning around. Fear turned to terror as he let his eyes drift down and saw the thick forearm crushing Morgan's windpipe and the knife at her throat. This man was tall, better-dressed, and had a scar that went from the corner of his mouth to his temple. His eyes would have been better suited to a snake. This was someone to be feared, he realised. No conscience, no empathy, just sheer evil intention.

Kidnapper number four. Noah swore as he walked around the annihilated counter and into the centre of the room.

'I'm going to walk her out of here and neither of you will get hurt.'

Moron, Noah thought. 'Do I look like I mind getting hurt? Let her go and *you* won't get hurt.'

A reptile smile to go with the reptile eyes. Noah expected to see a forked tongue at any moment. He flicked his glance to Morgan, who was looking at him, her gaze steady. Good girl—she wasn't panicking. He was close to it, he thought, as a drop of blood rolled down her neck and soaked into her T-shirt.

He'd cut her...

He was going to kill him for that.

'What do you want?' Noah demanded.

'Her, of course. Negotiations will be so much easier in Colombia if we have a bargaining chip.'

Noah shook his head. 'That's not going to happen. Where are the store employees?'

Snake-eyes shrugged. 'In the back. They might need medical care; we had to *persuade* them to call Miss Moreau down.'

Persuade as in beat the crap out of them to make them obey.

'We've been watching you for weeks—waiting for an opportunity. We couldn't afford to wait any more so we set a trap and you walked straight into it.'

Tell me about it. If one of his employees had done the same they'd be fired. He'd been distracted...by Morgan. *Maybe you shouldn't guard someone you want to sleep with...do you think, soldier?*

'I'm going to rip you apart,' Noah said.

And he would. That was a promise. Nobody threatened Morgan...ever.

'You okay there, Duchess?'

On cue she dropped like a stone, pulling Snake-eyes off-balance. Noah became a blur of speed, motion and deadly intent as he kicked the knife out of his hand and followed up with a lightning-fast punch to his stomach. Air whooshed out of his opponent as he sank to his knees.

Just to make sure that he had the upper hand, Noah wound his forearm around his neck and considered doing the specialised jerk that would send him into the ever after.

'You think you can put your grubby hands on my woman? Put a knife to her throat? Cut her?' he demanded, his voice rough.

He heard a faint gurgling and Morgan's desperate pleas from the other end of the long tunnel he was in. He continued to threaten his captor, tightening his grip with every word he spoke.

Morgan's hand smacking his head jerked him toward reality.

'The guy is turning blue! Let him go! You're going to kill him!'

Noah looked up at her, ignored her tear-filled eyes and shrugged. 'He hurt you. No one hurts you and gets away with it. You're bleeding.'

'It's a scratch, Noah. Look—the police are here. Let them take care of him.' Morgan slapped his head again. 'Let him go! *Now!* Please, Noah. Don't do this.'

Noah released the pressure and heard a couple of deep, rattling and relieved gurgles from his captor.

Noah felt sanity flowing back into him and withdrew his arm. He flipped the sleazoid over and smacked his head into the floor. *Oops...*

'Open the door, Duchess. And please tell them that I am one of the good guys and not to shoot me.'

Noah opened the door to Morgan's apartment and his hand on her back urged her into her home. She headed straight for her squishy couch and sank down onto the edge, staring at the multi-coloured Persian rug below her feet.

He was coming off the adrenalin high and was starting to feel every punch and kick he'd taken. He yanked his tie up and over his head and dropped it, very unusually for him, on the back of the couch. His lip was still bleeding and under the butterfly bandage the cut on his cheek was telling him—loudly—that it was there. His knuckles were bruised and bloody.

But Morgan was fine...mostly. Her neck was bruised from having that muscled arm applied to it, and there was a small nick on her neck from the knife. He kept looking at her to check that she hadn't developed another injury the EMTs might have overlooked.

'Sore?' Noah demanded when she touched her fingers to her throat.

'Mmm.' Morgan looked up at Noah's ravaged face and managed a smile. 'I'm fine, I promise.'

Noah crouched on his heels in front of her and rested his forehead on her knee. 'I thought I'd lost you, Morgan.'

Morgan lifted her hand to touch his cheek, letting her fingertips flutter just beneath the cut on his cheekbone. 'You're too good to lose anyone.'

'I was going to kill him,' Noah said. 'I lost control… *again.*'

'What do you mean?' She touched the deep frown between his brows. 'Noah? What's wrong?'

'Apart from the fact that you were nearly kidnapped and killed? That my heart stopped when I saw that knife to your neck?'

Morgan's eyes widened as his voice became louder with every word.

'That I nearly lost you and I can't lose anyone—ever again?'

'Okay, Noah, calm down.'

'I nearly got you killed in there because I wasn't concentrating!'

'Stop shouting! I'm pretty sure that people can hear you in the lobby.'

'You! Nearly! Died!'

Morgan shook her head. 'Yet here I still sit—alive, but starting to think that you're one crazy man. You were there. You saved me,' Morgan said, her eyes on his mouth. 'My real-life hero.'

'Don't call me that! It should never have happened,' Noah stated, his voice full of disgust. 'I walked you into an ambush…what was I thinking?'

'Stop beating yourself up… Oh, wait—someone already did that today.' Morgan's eyes and twitching mouth invited him to find his sense of humour.

'Ha-ha.'

Noah looked up into her beautiful eyes. His gaze travelled over her face and he winced at the small cut on her neck, the faint bruises on her throat. He'd already forgotten that his cheekbone was cut, that his bottom lip was split and puffy, that his body was battered and bruised.

She was okay. That was all that mattered. Life was too short and he knew that he could not go a minute more without making love to her. He needed her, craved her...emotions he found difficult to admit to. But he'd come so close to losing his life. And—far more scarily—her life.

Life, he decided, was too sweet to waste another minute denying himself the pleasure of making her his.

Noah's eyes darkened with passion and he couldn't resist any longer. When his lips met hers his tongue delved and danced and she responded, and he felt awed by the pent-up longing in her kiss. Unaware that his kisses were just as demanding, as urgent, he sucked in his breath when Morgan's hands moved to the bottom of his shirt, tugging it out of his jeans. Desperate to feel his flesh on hers, he moaned his frustration and resented the brief separation from her body as he stepped away from her to pull his shirt over his head.

Morgan leaned forward and ran her lips across his chest, stopping to flick her tongue over his nipple, to rub her cheek on his chest hair. Noah flipped open her shirt buttons and pulled the fabric apart, revealing her lacy pink bra and luscious chest to his gaze. She was so feminine, he thought. From her sense of humour to her resilience, her long legs and bold eyes, the texture and smell of her skin, she embodied all the traits that he'd spent his adult life looking for.

He finally—*finally!*—had his hands on her, and his imagination had fallen far short of the reality of how life-affirming touching her was. This time there would be no stopping him—stopping them. He needed her, had to have her, to be in her, around her, sharing this experience with her.

Noah felt Morgan's body soften, surrendering to the moment and to him. He bumbled through removing her clothes—suave he was *not*!—but eventually she lay back on the cushions, gloriously, stunningly naked except for the tiny scrap of flimsy lace that covered her crotch. He kept his eyes on her, planning which part of her luscious skin he'd suck on first—hard pink nipple, soft inner thigh?—as he quickly shed the rest of his clothing while Morgan watched him through heavy, half-closed eyes.

On a muttered curse, he reached for his discarded pants and pulled his wallet out of his back pocket. Scattering cards and cash, he found the condom he had taken to carrying around with him and ripped the top open with his teeth. He dropped the condom onto the table and he saw that Morgan was neither surprised nor shocked when he grabbed the flimsy material of her panties and snapped the thin bands that held the triangle in place. Her hand reached out to encircle his erection and he immediately rubbed himself against her most secret places, asking for her permission to enter. He wanted to take his time, to adore every inch of her body, but he'd waited for so long—weeks, years!

His fingers and his mouth followed where his erection had been, and under his touch Morgan surrendered, dissolved, just as he'd known she would. He knew the exact moment to pull back, when she could tolerate no more, so he lifted his head to adore her breasts with his mouth, tongue and lips.

Morgan patted the table, found the condom and stretched down to close her fingers around him. He relished the sound of her breathing, heavy in the quietness of the evening. The latex whispered over him, her fingers making the prosaic action the most erotic sexual play. Green eyes clashed with blue as she tugged him towards her, and he felt as if he'd come home when her softness wrapped around his solidity and enclosed him in her wet warmth. Noah slid one hand under her hip and the other cradled her head into his neck as he both encouraged her to ride with him and promised protection from the storm to follow. They were together.

Noah moved within her and Morgan followed. He demanded and Morgan responded. Deeper, longer, higher, faster. She met him stroke for stroke, matching his passion, glorying in her power. Then she shuddered, splintered. and through the swells of her climax Noah fractured with her.

It was heaven. It was home.

Emotionally, physically depleted, Noah pushed his face into Morgan's neck, breathed, sighed, and for the first time in far too long relaxed completely.

She was safe and she was his. Finally.

CHAPTER TEN

STELLENBOSCH, WESTERN CAPE. Home, Morgan thought as she flopped back onto the mattress of the canopied bed and groaned in delight. This was her favourite place in the entire world; the Bon Chance Wine Estate nestled into the mountains that embraced the family wine farm. This was where, as a child, she'd run wild with Riley and the children of the workers, all of them barefoot and dirty, their faces smeared with the juice of the mulberries they'd picked off the trees in the orchards, their pockets filled with the biscuits or mini-cakes Mariah, the cook, had tucked into their pockets.

On arrival, the kitchen had been the first place she'd headed to and there she'd been, her hair grey and her caramel face wrinkled, but her eyes shining with love.

After Mariah had met Noah and hugged James and Riley, and they'd all had a cup of her thick and strong stove-percolated coffee, she'd ushered them off to their rooms to freshen up—but not before tucking a large biscuit into Morgan's hand.

Morgan sat up, sat cross-legged on the bed under the antique wooden canopy and reached for the biscuit she'd placed on the side table.

'Are you going to share that?' Noah asked from where he stood in her open doorway.

Morgan waved him in as she bit down. 'No,' she said as the taste of vanilla and warm butter exploded on her tongue.

Noah walked in, took the biscuit from her hand and snapped it in half. He ignored her vociferous protests and popped it into his mouth. 'Damn it, that's good,' he said, after swallowing.

'Wait until you taste her pan-fried trout with almonds. That's on the menu for tonight.'

Noah walked over to the wooden sash window, placed his hands on the windowsill and looked out. 'It's so beautiful here, Morgan,' he stated quietly. 'The vines, the mountains...'

Morgan climbed off the bed and joined him at the window. 'Isn't it? This, more than any other place on earth, is my home. It's where we mostly grew up. A Moreau forefather bought this place in the late eighteen-hundreds, with the profits out of the first diamond mine they worked, but the house and winery date back to the beginning of the century.'

'The house is fantastic. From the moment you drive through those gates and up the oak-lined driveway you know that you are entering a place that's imbued with history. The white gables, the exposed wooden beams, the wooden floors. And, God, the furniture.'

Morgan looked amused. 'You've been around wealth before, soldier, why are you sounding so impressed?'

Noah gave her cheek the gentlest of flicks. 'I'm not impressed by wealth and you know it. It's the...*history*—the idea that your great-great-grandmother ate at that same table in the dining room that we will eat at tonight. It's the continuity of family...'

'Tell me about yours, Noah. Your family.'

Noah shook his head and his eyes hardened. 'The only thing to tell is that they are nothing like yours. Socially, economically, mentally...the other end of the spectrum' Noah looked around and raised his eye at the very luscious wooden canopy bed. 'And that is one heck of a bed. One might say that it is fit for a duchess.'

'If you play your cards right I might invite you into it.' Morgan batted her eyelashes at him.

'If you play your cards right I might say yes.' Noah batted his eyelashes back.

Morgan laughed and he grinned.

Noah stepped up to her, rested his temple against hers, his hands loose on her hips. 'James said that we're having a wine-tasting in the cellar in fifteen minutes, and as much as I want you I also want to take my time with you. Every waking moment during that interminable flight I spent planning what I intend to do with you...to you.'

Morgan licked her bottom lip as her hands drifted down over his stomach. 'Bet I could make a case for quick and fast now.'

Noah looked tempted, then swatted her on the backside before he walked away to the door. He gestured her through it 'Stop leading me into temptation and show me Bon Chance.'

Morgan grinned as she drifted past him in a cloud of mischief and expensive perfume. 'So you're admitting that I *can* lead you into temptation?'

'You know that you can,' Noah muttered, and placed his hand on her lower back to push her away from the bedrooms and towards the magnificent yellow wood staircase. 'Behave, Duchess.'

'But I'd so much rather *mis*behave...'

Noah hooked his arm around her neck and placed his hand over her mouth. 'Man, you're a pain in the ass.'

Morgan giggled as she placed her butt on the banister and slid down the stairs, landing on her feet in the hall. It was good to be home. And it was fabulous to be home with Noah.

Noah pushed open the massive oak door to Bon Chance and ushered Morgan through it, his hand on the centre of her back. She inhaled his sexy aftershave and held his arm as she slipped her sky-high open heels off her feet.

'I love this dress,' Noah stated, pulling the fabric of the

top layer of blush-pink silk organza between his finger and thumb and rubbing. The mini under-dress was a patchwork of different pinks...V neckline, black trim. She liked it, but judging by the gleam in Noah's eyes he couldn't wait to get her out of it.

Morgan tossed her clutch bag on the hall table, placed her hands on her back and stretched, pushing out her chest. She grinned when his eyes dropped and stayed on her chest.

Sometimes being a girl was the best fun ever—especially when you had a super-starry, sexy soldier looking at you with lust in his eyes.

'So, my friends weren't so bad, were they? You spent a lot of time talking to Jack and Luke,' Morgan commented.

Noah pulled his eyes up to her face. 'Uh...Jack knows my brother Mike. Journalist and photographer.'

'Small world.' Morgan glanced into the formal lounge. 'Do you want a nightcap? My dad likes a drop of Macallan every night.'

'My favourite whisky. Sounds good.'

Morgan walked in her bare feet into the lounge, shut the French doors behind her and opened a cabinet, revealing tumblers and a couple of bottles of whisky. 'There's an iPod on the shelf over there—do you want to choose some music?'

Morgan sighed when Sarah McLachlan's voice filled the room. Taking a glass over to Noah, she pressed the drink into his hand. She was about to step back when Noah's arms snaked around her waist and pulled her to him.

'No, stay here. Dance with me again.'

Morgan swayed on the spot with him and then took the glass out of his hand and took a sip. Anyone would think that she had never danced with a man before, yet never had she been so aroused this quickly. Standing up on her toes, she grazed his chin with her lips and slowly kissed his mouth. The music vibrated with desire, with love lost and found.

She heard the bang of crystal hitting wood and felt one of Noah's hands on her bottom, the other on the side of her face. Tongues tangled and hands rubbed at the restrictive barrier of clothing as the plaintive music faded into white noise. She groaned in the back of her throat as hearts clashed and tongues collided, stroked, duelled. One song drifted into another and Morgan murmured her dismay as Noah lifted his head and rested his forehead on hers. He tangled his fist in her hair and tipped her head up so that he could look into her sparkling eyes.

'I need you, Morgan. I know we shouldn't keep doing this...I promised your brother...'

'You saved my life. Trust me, you are James's new best friend—'

'But I still need you. Want you.'

'Then take me,' she whispered.

Her eyes drifted closed and her lips parted as she tipped her head to allow him access to her neck, to the very sensitive spot in the hollow of her throat. He pushed his hand up under her dress and lifted it. Easily, quickly, he found her nipple with his thumb. Morgan groaned, desperately wanting his lips and mouth to continue the exquisite torture. She slid her hand over his hip and stretched her hand so that she barely brushed his erection. It was a faint touch, but Morgan felt the electricity power through him. She felt strong and powerful, and she increased the pressure of her touch and had Noah moaning aloud.

Fumbling with the buttons on his shirt, Morgan eventually pulled the fabric apart and spread her hands over his chest, exploring his defined pecs and his washboard stomach. Pushing the shirt off his shoulders, she touched his collarbone with her tongue and inhaled the scent of his masculine skin.

'You're killing me here, lass. If you carry on like that it's not going to be slow and it's not going to be pretty.' Noah muttered.

'I never asked for either.'

Noah's hand skimmed her thigh and moved across her pelvis. His thumb rested on her mound and she groaned when it drifted lower, yelped when he hit the spot.

'It would be easier if we just got naked,' Noah replied, spinning her around and looking for the zip that held her dress together. Morgan felt cool air on her back and sighed when Noah's hot mouth touched her spine as her dress dropped. His big hands reached around to clasp her breasts and his fingers pulled her nipples into rock-hard points.

This was better than she could have imagined. Noah unclasped her bra and it fell to the floor in a pretty puddle of pink froth, and then her panties were pushed down her legs and she stood naked, her back to his chest, his lips on her neck.

'You're so beautiful.'

Noah turned her around and watched her with lowered lust-filled eyes as he dropped his hands to undo his belt. Morgan gripped the back of the antique couch and licked her lips as he pushed his pants down his legs, standing in front of her in a pair of plain black tight trunks, strained by his very impressive erection.

Two seconds later his trunks were on the floor, his hands were under her thighs and he was lifting her up, his penis probing her slick, wet folds. He held her eyes as he surged into her. He was hard and wonderful and her body shuddered.

'So wet...so warm.'

Morgan moaned as she linked her arms around his strong neck. Her clitoris brushed against his groin as he pulled her even closer and she moaned and tipped her head back. She ground herself into him as Noah looked for and found her mouth. His tongue swirled and slid as he pumped his hips. Morgan groaned as she felt the fierce upward swing of concentrated pleasure...reaching out for that dizzying release... She lifted her hips and mashed herself against him.

'Take it, baby. Use it,' Noah said, his voice low and intense in her ear. 'Use me! Take it all.'

She was all feeling, all concentrated pleasure, as she did

what he said. She bucked and pumped, sinking into him and then using her hands against the couch to push up and away from him so that she could crash down on him again. Power and release built as her body became a vessel of shimmying, sensational pleasure.

Reaching, reaching, and then bursting, flying, Morgan flung her arms around Noah's neck and held on as she split into a thousand pieces and was tacked back together with fairy dust. Somewhere, somehow, she knew that Noah had followed her over the edge; she could hear him panting in her ear, could feel the aftershocks rippling through his muscles, the slight softening of his erection inside her.

Morgan lost track of time; she wasn't sure how long she sat there, half supported by the couch, half by Noah's bulging-with-muscles arms. But eventually Noah slid out of her and held her as her feet touched the floor, holding her arm to make sure that she was steady.

Noah brushed her hair back from her face. 'You okay?'

'Good. Really, really good,' Morgan said on a yawn. 'Boneless.'

Noah picked up his pants, stepped into them and tucked himself away as he did up the fly. 'Let's get you dressed and into bed.'

Noah picked up her dress and she shimmied it over her head. Picking up their underwear, he shoved it into his pockets and picked up his shoes. Taking Morgan's hand, he pulled her towards the French doors.

'Upstairs.'

'I don't think I have the energy to climb those stairs.' Morgan looked at the stairs doubtfully. 'I'm utterly exhausted.'

Noah bent his knees, grabbed her around the thighs and tossed her over his shoulder. Morgan squealed and laughed and slapped his back. 'I was joking, Noah! Put me down.'

'I live to serve, Duchess. Stop wriggling or I will drop you on your imperial ass.'

* * *

Morgan woke up late and rolled over in her massive bed, looking for Noah. Not finding any part of his masculine bod in her bed, she sat up and scowled. He'd sneaked out, the rat, after a night spent exploring her in the most intimate ways possible. He'd reached for her time and time again and they had only drifted off to sleep when the sun had started to yawn, allowing its weak early-morning rays to drift over the mountain.

Being with him had been—bar none and by far—the best sex of her life. The sexy, slightly stand-offish soldier was an amazing lover: demanding, adoring, creative. He hadn't allowed her to feel any modesty and had encouraged her to be forthright and honest. She'd felt comfortable telling him what she liked and didn't like him doing.

There hadn't been any 'getting to know you' or 'wanting to impress you' sex. It had been down and dirty—more like 'I want to know how far I can push you' sex.

More like the type of sex people had when they had known each other a while and were really comfortable in bed together. Weird and astonishing for their first few times together.

Morgan glanced at the clock. It was just past nine and, while she could easily roll over and go back to sleep, she wanted to be with Noah, here in her most favourite spot in the world.

Morgan pushed back the covers and padded over to the en-suite bathroom. Hearing muted voices in the passageway, she cocked her head. Riley and...her brother? What was James doing on this side of the passage? His room and study were on the other wing of the house—to the right of the staircase and not to the left.

Curious, she padded on tiptoe to the door and cracked it open. Her eyes widened as she saw James, still dressed in the pants he'd worn to the wedding and with his smart grey shirt bunched in his hand.

'If you say it was a mistake, I swear I'll stab you with…
something,' Riley hissed.

'Dammit, Riley, you are like my—'

Morgan put her hand against her mouth to stifle her laughter as Riley, obviously naked beneath a silky short robe, plastered her mouth against James's and slapped her hands on his butt. She kissed him thoroughly and with some skill, Morgan noticed, and when they came up for air James looked shell-shocked.

'You didn't say that when you were moaning my name in the throes of passion last night.'

'Ri—okay. But—'

'I am not your sister or your friend. And I'm done pining away for you. You have ten seconds to decide if you want to explore this heat we have always had or whether you are walking away for good. But you should know that if you walk that's it. You don't get a second chance.'

'Riley, I—'

'Ten seconds, nine, eight, seven—'

'It's not that easy.'

Yes, it is, you ass! Morgan wanted to shout. *She's the best thing that ever happened to you!*

'Six, five, four, three…'

Morgan bit her lip as her best friend counted down and her stupid brother just stared at her with miserable eyes. Morgan closed her own eyes at the immense pain she saw in Riley's before the door closed in James's face.

Morgan fought the urge to step into the passage and slap some sense into James. She knew it wouldn't help. James was as stubborn as she was—maybe more. She couldn't help him see what was right in front of his face; couldn't force him to feel love when he didn't.

Morgan watched him walk down the passage and then glanced to Riley's closed door. To knock or not to knock? Normally she would just barge in there and offer comfort, curse her brother just to make Riley smile. But she suspected that this went too deep, meant too much, and her gut instinct was to leave Riley alone. She would reach out when she could and when she was ready to.

In the meantime she had her own six-foot-three man to find.

Morgan, dressed in a very brief pair of faded denim shorts, flip-flops and a tank top—early autumn in South Africa still spiked the temperatures to boiling—took the cup of coffee Mariah poured her and with a muffin in her hand walked out through the back door of the house. Mariah had said that she'd seen Noah walk in the direction of the southside vines and the dam, and that was nearly an hour ago.

Morgan, munching on her cheese and spinach muffin and sipping her coffee, tipped her face to the sun and pulled in deep breaths of fresh mountain air. She wished that they weren't flying out later tonight, that she and Noah could hang out here a bit longer. There was no security threat, no pollution, no crazy traffic, no boring functions to attend, no ball to organise. It was impossible, but it was a lovely dream to indulge in as she looked for her lover-slash-bodyguard.

Morgan dusted her hands against the seat of her pants to get rid of the crumbs and waved to some labourers working the vines.

And there he was, Morgan thought, sitting on the edge of the dam, his arms loosely linked around his knees, his dark hair glinting in the sun. He hadn't shaved and his stubble gave him a rugged look that had her mouth watering. Warmth pooled between her legs as she remembered the feel of those back muscles that red T-shirt covered, the hard butt underneath his cotton shorts. He was beautiful: masculine grace wrapping a fantastically loyal spirit and a sharp brain.

Morgan approached him quietly, covered his eyes with her hands and whispered in his ear. 'Guess who?'

Noah didn't say anything. He just pulled her hands down

and held her arms so that she was plastered against his back, her head next to his, her breasts mashed into his chest.

'You okay, Noah?' she asked quietly. 'What's going on in that head of yours, soldier?'

A part of him—a big part of him—wished he could open up, just release all this churned-up emotion inside him. He wanted to tell her that he couldn't decide whether he regretted sleeping with her or not…that being with her had been everything he'd dreamt of and more and also, on the other hand, his biggest nightmare. He'd lost himself in her body, had adored every minute of her, and he mourned his lack of self-control as he'd lost himself in her. He wanted to tell her that when she'd drifted off in the early hours of this morning he'd just lain next to her and watched her breathe.

She'd decimated him with her soft lips, her whispered moans, her delicate hands on his not-so-delicate body. She'd touched his heart with her murmurs of delight, her whispers of gratitude at the way he made her feel, and his heart had swelled when he'd heard his name on her lips as he tipped her over into orgasm time and time again.

But on the flipside of the coin he hadn't even started to think what effect sleeping with her would have on his job, on his ability to keep her safe. They'd caught four more kidnappers but another gang could be contracted tomorrow. Until the situation in Colombia was definitively resolved she wouldn't be completely safe, so he would remain in place as her bodyguard. Would thoughts of what they did to and with each other distract him if something else happened? Would he be less sharp, less aware, less able to say no to her when she wanted to do something or be somewhere that could place her in danger?

Morgan pulled her hands out of his grasp and sat down beside him on the grassy bank, staring at the water. Now and again the water rippled as a trout broke the surface to look for food. In another life he could imagine being here with Morgan, casting a fly while she lazed on the bank, a glass of wine in her hand.

Noah leaned back on his hands and looked past the dam to the vines in their perfect rows, and from there to the purple-blue mountain looming over the farm. 'It's such a stunning place, Morgs. I can't understand why you're in New York when you can be here.'

'Clients, mostly. But I should take more time to come back here.' Morgan pushed her hair behind her ears. Then she placed her palm on Noah's thigh, gently squeezed and lifted it again. 'Please don't regret what happened between us, Noah. It was too good for regrets.'

'It's so complicated, Morgan,' he said in a gruff voice.

'I think you make it a great deal more complicated than it is,' Morgan replied. 'We're friends who have shared our bodies. We had a great deal of fun, and if we do it again we'll have fun again.'

Noah frowned. 'So, you're not looking forward? Expecting anything from me?'

Morgan crossed her legs, picked a blade of grass and ran it through her fingers. 'I was talking to Riley about this a little while ago, and spending more time with you has just reinforced my opinion that I'm not cut out to be with someone long-term.'

Noah frowned, utterly confused. 'Why not?'

'I've shielded you from my dyslexia—shielded you from what I go through on a daily basis. I shield everyone. I never read the news; I watch it. I try to avoid writing anything down because my handwriting looks like a chicken's scrawl and I can't spell. At all. I don't drive unless I know exactly where I am and the route I'm travelling, and I never drive in New York or any other city.'

'Okay.'

'On the few occasions I do write something on the computer I call Riley to check the spelling.'

'Um...spellcheck?' Noah volunteered.

'It doesn't help if you don't recognise the word, Noah.'

Oh, flip. He hadn't thought of that.

'Look, I've done tons of research on dyslexia and there are a couple of things I can't wrap my head around. Both of them involve a steady relationship. One is that if I get involved then I can't do it halfway. I'd want the whole bang-shoot. Marriage, kids…everything. Having kids is a risk, because dyslexia is hereditary and I couldn't bear it if my husband blamed me for his child struggling at school. The other is that one day, as hard as I will try to prevent it, my partner will feel frustrated with me and then disappointed. Quickly followed by him thinking that, despite how hard we've tried, something is lacking. In me.'

Noah stared at her profile for a long, long time before pulling in a deep breath. He looked for the right words but only two hovered on his tongue. 'Horse crap, Morgan.'

'Excuse me?' she gasped, shocked.

'That is the biggest load of self-indulgent horse crap I've ever heard—' Noah cursed as his mobile disturbed the country silence of the morning. He pulled out his mobile, checked the display and frowned. 'Sorry, it's my father's carer. I need to take this.'

As the feminine Scottish lilt travelled across the miles, giving him news he didn't want to hear, Noah felt the world shift under his feet. He dropped the phone to the grass and bent his head as he struggled to make sense of her words.

Fell out of his wheelchair. Hit his head. Bleeding on the brain. Dead…

'Noah?'

He felt Morgan's cool hand on his cheek.

'Hon, what's happened?'

'He's dead. He's finally dead.' Noah heard the words but his brain had no connection to the words his tongue was speaking. 'I thought I'd be happier.'

'Who's dead, Noah?'

'My father.' He ran his hand over his face. 'I have to go

to Scotland. I have to tell my brothers. Man, can't we just go back to our conversation? I want to tell you why I thought you were talking rubbish. It doesn't have to be like that...'

The trees were dancing and the water in the dam was rising and falling. What was happening to him?

Morgan gripped his hands. 'Just breathe, Noah. In and out.'

'So many times I wished he was dead, and now he is and I don't know what to feel.' Noah stared at the sky. 'I need to go, Morgan. I need to tell my brothers.'

He heard his irrational gabbling and felt embarrassed. He never gabbled...wasn't irrational.

'You will tell them, Noah. Just breathe for now, take in the news, stop thinking and let yourself feel.'

Noah shook his head and jumped to his feet. *Hell, no!* The last thing he wanted or needed to do was feel.

Morgan followed him up, placed her hands on his chest and looked up into his ravaged face. 'Noah, stop. Listen to me—no, don't push past me! You're as white as a sheet. *Listen* to me!'

Noah forced himself to concentrate on her words.

'I'm going to walk away and you are going to sit down and take it in. Take a deep breath and look around. You've just heard that your father is dead. Take a moment. Feel. Cry. Do what you need to do. There's going to be a time when you need to be strong, and the next fifteen minutes, half an hour—the rest of the day if that's what you need—isn't that time.' Morgan touched his cheek with her fingers. 'Take the time, Noah. Please.'

Noah saw the sympathy in her eyes and bit his lip, fighting the emotion that was threatening to crash over him. If she had let him walk, do what he needed to do, he could have pushed it away, but if he had to stay here then he didn't want her seeing the mess he would probably dissolve into. The anger, the regret, the swamping, swamping guilt.

'Go.' Noah muttered the word, shoving his hand into his hair. 'Go now.'

Morgan nodded once, then bent down, quickly scooped up his mobile and tucked it into her pocket. He watched her walk away and it was only when she was out of sight that he allowed the first hot, angry, guilty wave of emotion to crash over him.

CHAPTER ELEVEN

MORGAN WALKED FROM the galley area of the jet and sat down next to Noah, who was staring out at the solid black expanse that was the African continent below them. She pressed a whisky into his hand and put her temple on his shoulder. 'How are you doing, soldier?'

Noah took a sip, shuddered, and gestured to the window. 'I never realised how dark Africa really is. You hardly ever see lights.'

So, not ready to talk, then.

'Just miles and miles of nothingness,' Morgan agreed, tucking her feet up under her. She'd shed her shoes earlier and she reached for the soft blanket that she'd put on the chairs opposite them and pulled it over her knees.

'Cold?' Noah asked, slipping his arm around her and pulling her closer.

'A little.'

Noah kissed her hair before taking another sip of his whisky. 'I never expected you to commandeer the family jet to take me to London, Morgan.'

'It was James's suggestion, Noah. I'm sorry we couldn't leave earlier, but they were doing some maintenance on it.' Morgan replied.

James had been quick to offer the use of the plane, saying that the jet could turn around in London and come back to pick them up. So they'd return to New York a day later? The world wouldn't stop. Morgan knew that there was a reason why she adored her brother. It made it hard to remain annoyed with him over the hurting-Riley issue.

'It's an expensive exercise, Morgan. I could've just caught a normal flight. And I didn't expect you to come with me. I was going to send another operative to guard you while I was away.'

'I don't want to train someone else,' Morgan joked, and then sighed at his worried eyes and his serious face. 'Noah, relax. We're hugely rich and we can afford to send the jet anywhere we want, whenever we want. We wanted to get you to London in the quickest, most comfortable way possible. I wanted to be with you because I don't think that anybody should be alone at a time like this.'

Noah kissed her head again. 'I'm not used to people doing stuff for me.'

'Yeah, I realised that. Talking of which, James contacted Chris and gave him a heads-up. He'll meet you at the airport with another guard for me and I'll let you do what you need to do. I'd like to stay with you, but that might not be what you want.'

Noah was silent for a long time and Morgan subdued her pang of disappointment. Of course he didn't want to have to worry about her at a time like this... Yeah, they had slept together, but that didn't mean he wanted her to invade his emotional space.

'When you're done—when the funeral is over—the jet will take us back to New York. That's if you're coming back with me.'

Noah rubbed his eyes. 'It's so difficult to think. To decide what to do next.'

Morgan placed her hand on his thigh and left it there. 'I know... Well, I don't know, but I can imagine.'

'My brothers—'

Morgan remembered the comment he'd made at the art

exhibition. 'As much as you want to, you can't shield them from this, Noah.'

'Yeah.' Noah turned his head to look out of the window again into the black nothingness.

She'd never known anyone who needed someone to release what was obviously years of pent-up emotion more than he did. She knew that there was a huge and possibly tragic story here—that Noah was dealing with far more than just—*just!*—the death of his dad. Morgan wished she could shake it out of him, but she also suspected that she was the last person he'd allow to peek into his soul.

He saw himself as the protector, the guardian, but he didn't realise that in order to give you had to be able to receive. That you had to be strong enough—physically, mentally, *emotionally*—to do that. She worried about him... worried that as soon as the plane landed he would be all business in a 'let's-get-this-done-and-sorted' mode. She didn't know much about death but she knew that he had to grieve, had to mourn. He couldn't keep tamping down his emotion because one day he would erupt and splatter.

But this wasn't her party and she couldn't make him cry if she wanted to. All she could do was to be here, offering her unconditional support.

'We were raised in a bad area of Glasgow,' Noah said, his accent broad and his voice low.

He was still staring out of the window and Morgan didn't move a muscle, scared that he'd stop talking if she reacted at all. 'My father was frequently out of work. He had few skills and no desire to get any more. He lived off the dole and drank most of it away. My mum took whatever work she could find and kept him under control—mostly. He was an angry man and liked being that way.'

Morgan pushed her shoulder into his, pushed her fingers into his hand and kept her silence.

'My mum wanted to move out; she could get a job in her brother's inn in Kelso. He didn't want to move but she finally persuaded him to visit with her. They borrowed a car and my brothers and I stayed behind—I can't remember why. My father wasn't an experienced driver and it was wet and they spun off the road. Mum was killed instantly. Michael was paralysed from the waist down.'

Michael, he called his father Michael. Not Dad—just Michael.

'Long story short: he became our worst nightmare. Anger turned to rage, rage to violence, and if you think a man can't be physically violent confined to a wheelchair then you should've seen him. I watched my brothers become walking robots, scared to move—to breathe—and I called Social Services, They arranged for them to go and live with my aunt—my mum's sister.'

'And you?'

'Somebody had to stay and look after him. I lasted three years,' Noah said. 'I was nineteen when I joined up.'

'What happened that made you leave?' Morgan asked, because she knew that something major had happened. Noah, being Noah, with his unquestionable loyalty, would have had to have an excellent reason to walk away.

Still looking out of the window, he said, 'I said he was abusive and he was. Verbally, physically… But that day had been a quiet day—no drama from him. He'd actually been behaving himself. I walked past him and saw this cold look in his eye, and then his fist flew out and he punched me in my…you know…'

Morgan's eyes widened but she kept her voice even. 'Groin?'

'Yeah. I just reacted. We were in the kitchen and…I don't know what happened but I lost time. When I came back I was holding a knife to his throat and he was begging me not to kill him. I wanted to; it would've been so easy.'

'But you didn't.'

'No, I walked away, made arrangements for his care and joined the army. I left him alone.'

Morgan turned to face him, lifted up her hand and touched his chin, forcing him to look at her. 'You spent three years in a horrid situation with an abusive father. You earned the right to walk away, Noah. Knowing you, you've probably supported him financially all this time.'

'Yes, I have—but you don't understand!' Noah sounded agitated. 'I nearly *killed* him, Morgan!'

Morgan raised her eyebrows. 'But you *didn't*, Noah! He was an abusive father who inflicted violence on you. He sucker-punched you—in a man's most vulnerable place!—and it was the straw that broke your back. I'm surprised that you *didn't* kill him, Noah.'

'You don't understand! I lost control! Like I nearly did the other day.'

'Oh, Noah, millions of men would think that you showed immense control by *not* killing him! And you were nowhere near losing control last week.'

Noah looked at her with wide shocked eyes and she could see him trying to process her words. 'Have you ever spoken to anyone about this? Chris? Your brothers? A psychologist?'

Noah shook his head.

She was the only person that knew his secret? How could that be? 'Maybe you should. Maybe they can convince you that you were just a boy, trying to survive and doing the best you could in a dreadful situation.'

Noah closed his eyes and rested his head on hers. 'I'm so tired, Morgs.'

Morgan pushed his hair off his forehead. 'Then why don't you rest awhile? Push the seat back and try and sleep, okay?' Morgan pulled the lever on his seat and watched as he stretched out. She passed him a pillow, pulled another blanket over him, before flipping her seat back and lying so that she faced him. Holding his hand, she watched as he drifted off to sleep.

'Morgs?'

'Yes?'

He yawned and his voice was thick with sleep when he spoke again. 'Stay with me, okay? I'd like you there…at the funeral and when I tell my brothers.'

'I'll be there,' Morgan whispered, and watched him while he slept.

Noah was as jittery as a crack addict desperate for a fix. He stood in front of one of the many houses in the grimy brick block and placed his hand on the incongruous red railing—and quickly lifted it when he felt the sticky gunge on his skin. Wiping his palm on his jeans, he played with the keys in his hand.

He hadn't been back to the house he'd been raised in in nearly fifteen years and he didn't want to go inside now. He just wanted to put this entire nightmare behind him. But before he could he had to bury his father tomorrow and clean out his house today. Postponing wasn't an option, because his brothers were flying in later and would insist on helping him. Their aunt's house was their real home, and he didn't want them to see the reality of how their parents had lived.

He didn't want Morgan seeing it either, but she wouldn't be dissuaded from accompanying him. He'd pleaded for her to stay in the hotel room, had offered another bodyguard for the day so that she could spend the day sightseeing, but she'd refused.

She was coming with him and he'd have to deal with it, she'd stated, calmly and resolutely. Nobody should have to clear out their parents' house alone.

He wasn't sure whether to be grateful or to strangle her. He looked over to her, dressed as he was in old jeans and a casual sweater. But she still looked out of place in this place of dank and dark buildings covered in grime and graffiti.

Over the past day or so Morgan's presence had kept him centred, grounded, able to go through the steps of organising the funeral, notifying the few relatives they had left, and that hard conversation with his brothers, who'd taken the news rather prosaically. He couldn't judge them for their lack of grief; they'd had minimal contact with Michael for most of their lives and didn't have a personal relationship with him. He also knew that their offer to come to the funeral was more to support him than to say goodbye to their father.

Yesterday, after a long, cold, tough day, he'd lost himself in Morgan's body, stepping away from the memories of the past and the reality of his father's passing and losing himself in her smooth skin, her frantic gasps, her warm, wet heat. And when guilt had welled up and threatened to consume him whole, when he'd felt like punching a fist through a wall, her words, spoken quietly but with such truth, drifted through his head.

'Millions of men would think that you showed immense control by not *killing him. You were just a boy, trying to survive and doing the best you could in a dreadful situation.'*

Morgan. She was becoming as necessary to him as breathing and he either wanted to beg her never to leave him or he wanted to run as far and as fast away from her as possible.

Noah saw movement across the road and caught the eye of the obvious leader of a gang of teens across the road. He gave them a don't-mess-with-me stare. They ducked their heads and moved off and Noah sighed. *There but for the grace of God go I,* he'd thought, on more than one occasion.

'Let's go in, Noah, it's cold out here,' Morgan suggested, her hand on his back.

Noah shook himself out of his trance and walked up the cracked steps into the mouldy building. He shuddered as he breathed in the smell of decaying food and despair.

He automatically turned to the door on the left and his hand shook as he tried to place the key in the lock. He didn't know why they bothered with locking up; he knew that one solid kick would have the door flying open. When he couldn't make the connection between key and lock he considered it a viable option.

Morgan took the key from his hand, jabbed it in the lock

and pushed open the door. She stepped inside and Noah wanted to warn her not to...that his father was unstable, volatile, capricious.

No, his father was dead. Noah bit his bottom lip, looked around and swore. Nothing had changed; the old blue couch was just paler and grubbier, the furniture that much more battered. And, man, it was messy. His father had always been a slob but Noah had paid for a cleaner, for someone to look after him.

'How did he live like this?' Noah whispered. 'If the carer didn't clean, then did she feed him, look after him?'

Guilt threatened to buckle his knees, sink him to the floor.

Morgan tossed him a glance and immediately went to the old fridge, yanked it open. She pulled back at the smell but pointed out the milk, the cheese. Slamming the door shut, she pulled open the freezer section and nodded.

'There are quite a few homemade meals in here, Noah, and lots of dirty dishes in the sink. He was eating. And, look, there's a note on the fridge, saying that the carer was going on holiday. She got back the day he died. I think.'

'Thank you.' Noah looked down as he kicked a half-empty bottle of whisky at his feet. So the drinking hadn't stopped.

He couldn't do this with her here... Couldn't handle seeing his classy NYC girl in a smelly flat filled with dirty dishes and soiled clothes and windows covered with soot and grime. Couldn't handle the pity he thought he saw in her eyes. He wanted to cry but he couldn't do that with her— couldn't let her see him at his weakest.

'Morgan, please leave.'

Morgan looked at him with huge eyes. 'I don't want to. I don't want you to do this on your own. Let me stay, please.'

Noah dropped his head and felt the walls of the room closing in on him. He desperately wanted to be alone, wanted some time to himself, to sort through the emotion to find the truth of what he was feeling. He knew it was time to pull away from her now, to find some distance. He wanted to take back his life, his mind, his control. He wanted to stand alone, as he always had. He needed to know that he could, that he didn't need that gorgeous blonde in his life, standing in his corner.

Why had he even explained his past to Morgan? Where had that crazy impulse come from? Being side-winded after hearing that Michael was dead? Now he felt as if he was standing in front of her, his chest cracked open, and inviting her to wreak havoc. By allowing her inside he'd handed her his pistol and invited her to shoot him in the heart.

He was the closest he'd ever come to falling over that long cliff into love, and he couldn't help thinking whether he would be feeling the same way if his father hadn't died— if his feelings for her didn't seem deeper because there was so much emotion swirling around him.

He just wanted to step away from this freakin' soul-searching and get on an even keel again. He wanted to feel normal.

Morgan folded her arms across her chest. 'Talk to me, Noah. Please.'

'You're not going to like what I say,' he warned her.

'Talk to me anyway,' Morgan said, perching her butt on the side of the rickety dining room table. She stood in nearly the same place as he had when he'd taken a knife to his father's throat...

He stared at the old television screen. 'My parents are both dead and I should feel free. Except that I don't.'

'Why not?'

'Because you're here.'

'Do you want to explain that?'

Noah shoved his hand into his hair and tugged. 'I don't want you to think that just because you're here we have something serious happening. I don't want you thinking that we're in some sort of relationship...'

'We are. If nothing else, we are friends.'

'Friends?'

Noah snorted, thinking that by allowing her to come with him he'd tied himself to Morgan, bound himself into some sort of relationship. He was furious that she'd pricked through his self-sufficiency and made him rely on her.

He looked around the room and felt anger whirl and swirl. 'I left this place fifteen years ago and I swore that I would never feel vulnerable again. I vowed, after walking away from him, that I'd never feel weak again.'

Yet here he was, shortly before burying the person who'd taught him that lesson, putting himself in the same position. With her.

He was such a fool. He couldn't, *wouldn't* ever rely on someone else again...and this touchy-feely crap he had going on with Morgan stopped now.

'I don't want you here. I want you gone.'

Had he actually voiced those words? He must have because her head jerked back in shock and all colour drained from her face.

'Noah...'

'This—you and I—it stops. Right now.'

'You're tired and upset and not thinking straight,' Morgan said after a moment, and he could see that she was trying to keep calm, desperately looking to keep the conversation, the situation, rational.

In normal circumstances her words might have jerked him back to sanity, but nothing about standing in his father's filthy house, being bombarded with ugly memories and emotions, was normal. If he wasn't in such a turbulent mood he'd readily admit that when it came to him she generally knew exactly what to say. How to make him laugh, think, want her with every breath he took.

He didn't *want* to want her like this; didn't want to deal with the tender emotions only she could pull to the surface. Didn't want to deal with anything right now...

'Why don't I give you some space?' Morgan sucked in her cheeks. 'I'll wait for you outside.'

Morgan turned to walk to the door but his harsh voice had her stopping just before she reached it. 'No. I don't want you to wait. I don't want this—you—any more.'

He saw, maybe felt the shudder that rocketed through her, saw her head fall. He fought the urge to go to her, to soothe, to protect. The child in him protested that *he'd* never been soothed, protected.

'I never promised you anything and I always said that I would leave.'

Morgan finally turned around, lifted her head and gave him a withering look. 'Stop acting like an ass, Noah. I understand that this has been a rough time for you, but don't take your anger out on the people who love you.'

Noah leaned backed and stretched out his feet. 'So now you *love* me?'

Morgan's eyes froze. 'I'm not even going to dignify that with a reply. You're angry and hurt and acting like a jerk. You're just going through the stages of grief—albeit quicker than most. First shock, you skipped denial. and now you're feeling angry.'

'No, you're looking for an excuse because you don't want to hear what I'm saying.'

'Which is exactly what, Noah? Put your cards on the table, Fraser.'

Well, okay, then. 'I don't want you in my life any more.'

'That's not how you felt this morning, last night, twenty minutes ago.'

That was the truth.

'It's how I feel now. I don't like feeling this connected to someone—feeling like my heart wants to explode with joy just because you're in the room. I want to feel normal again—me again… Not a twisted-with-emotion sap.' Noah ground the words out, forcing them around his reluctant tongue. 'I don't want to love you! And I certainly don't need you. I was perfectly fine on my own.'

He hadn't been, his heart shouted, but he shut out its screams.

Morgan shook her head, blinked away the emotion in her eyes and bit her bottom lip. He felt lower than an amoeba infected with anthrax. What was wrong with him? He was tossing away the best thing in his life...*ever*.

'Well, that was very clear.'

Morgan lifted her chin and he had to admire her courage.

'Well, screw you and your lousy, spiteful, wimpy attitude.' She grabbed her bag off the table and yanked it over her shoulder. 'I'm going back to the hotel.'

Noah watched her take a couple of steps before remembering that she was still a target, Glasgow or not. 'You can't leave by yourself!' he shouted.

Morgan bared her teeth at him and he was quite sure that her eyes were glowing red. He couldn't blame her.

'Watch me. I'd rather be kidnapped by rabid Colombians than spend one more minute with you!'

Noah stood up, pulled out his mobile and nodded, his face grim. 'That's easy to make happen.' Pushing buttons, he held it up to his ear, and his voice was rough when he spoke. 'Amanda?' He waited a minute before speaking again. 'Listen, I know that we've had our problems but do you have any agents in Glasgow who can take over Morgan Moreau's protection detail?' He waited a beat and spoke again. 'No, I need him now. Like within the next half-hour...hour. You have? Great.'

Noah rattled off the address and bit his lip. 'Thanks. Amanda. I think the threat level to her has mostly been neutralised. but tell him that if anything happens to her—if she breaks even a fingernail—he's dead.'

Noah disconnected the call and slapped his mobile against the palm of his hand. He looked at Morgan, whose eyes were wide with shock, humiliation and hurt. He wanted to take her in his arms, apologise, but he knew that the smarter course of action would be to walk away from her while he still could. While his heart was still his and not walking around in her hands.

'Your wish is my command, Duchess,' he said with a mocking bow.

Now he just had to keep himself from hitting redial, cancelling the new bodyguard, gathering Morgan up and keeping her for ever.

It was the longest, quietest, hardest, most excruciating wait of his life, and when she walked out to the car with a kid who looked as if he should still be in school he stood in his old house, sank to the couch and, for the first time in fifteen years, cried.

CHAPTER TWELVE

A WEEK LATER Riley walked into Morgan's studio, two cups in her hand, and Morgan sighed at the green logo of the twin-tailed mermaid on the cup. It was a mega hazelnut-flavoured latte, her favourite, and she needed it—along with Prozac and probably a padded cell.

'Hey, I was just about to buzz you,' Morgan said. 'I need help.'

'Okay.' Riley took a seat on the stool next to her at the workbench. 'You look like hell. Still crying?'

Morgan took a deep breath and nodded. 'Yeah. You?'

'Mmm... What a pair we are. You've heard the news?'

'That James is on his way back from Colombia and a deal is imminent?'

'Yeah.'

Morgan sighed and pointed out a word on her computer screen. 'What's this word?'

Riley bent down and peered over her shoulder. 'Vichyssoise.'

'Jeez, I can't read in English and they throw French words in,' Morgan grumbled. 'Do you have some time? Can you go through this menu for the ball with me?'

'Sure.'

She and Riley spent the next fifteen minutes discussing the ball, finalising the menu and the entertainment, the decorations and the ticket sales—which were going through the roof.

'We also need to approve the design of the mannequin cages and we need Noah's input there.'

Morgan stared at her fingers. 'Feel free to call him. I won't.'

She felt the tears in the back of her throat. His words from a week ago still bounced around her skull.

'I don't want you here any more.'

He'd preferred to face his demons alone than have her around. What did that say about her? She could understand him dumping her when they got back to New York, when he got bored with the sex, but she'd seen how much pain he'd been in, how he'd been struggling to deal with the memories of his past, and she'd thought that he'd want her there—that he wouldn't want to go through that alone.

But, no, Noah hadn't wanted her around.

All her life she'd tried to be good enough—for her family, for herself. She knew that she didn't always reach the standard she'd set for herself, and mostly she was okay with that. But to be told, during such a sad time, that she wasn't wanted or needed had lashed her soul.

She simply wasn't good enough…

'Horse crap, Morgan.'

She heard Noah's words spoken at Bon Chance as clear as day and actually looked around for the source of that statement. When Riley didn't react she looked inside herself and heard the phrase again.

'The biggest, load of self-indulgent horse crap.'

Morgan almost laughed as emotion swelled inside her. She wasn't sure where it came from, what its source was, but she recognised the power of it, saw the pure truth for the first time in a week, months—her entire life.

'Bats on a freakin' broomstick,' she muttered.

'Pardon?' Riley looked up and frowned.

Morgan looked at her best friend and put her hand over

her mouth in surprised shock. 'What happened with Noah wasn't about me...it was about *him*.'

'Okay, I have no idea what you're talking about,' Riley complained.

'Him kicking me into touch wasn't about me—wasn't about me not being good enough. I just assumed it was because I always assume the worst about myself. I keep saying that it's hard for people to deal with my dyslexia. but in truth I've never come to terms with it. And because of that I assume that everything is about me. My habitual reaction is to think that I'm not good enough, to think the worst of myself.'

Riley leaned back and clapped a slow beat. 'Well, glory hallelujah, the child has seen the light.'

Morgan stood up and paced the area in front of Riley. 'He told me what the problem was but I didn't listen. He said that he didn't like feeling so connected to me—something about his heart and feeling joy when I was around. That around me emotion twisted him up.' Morgan pointed her finger at Riley. '*He's* the one who's scared, who doesn't know what to do with me. He felt insecure and emotional and... Damn it, I'm going to smack him into next year!'

Riley smiled. 'I'd like to see you try.'

'He was hurting and not knowing why he was grieving for his father—the man was a waste of oxygen by all accounts—he didn't know how to channel his emotion and he lashed out. He needed me, but he was scared to need me. Everyone else he needed had either left him or let him down. He had to push me away to protect himself.'

'Look at you—you're a female Dr Phil.' Riley crossed her legs. 'So, what are you going to do, Morgs?'

'Go to him, of course. I might understand better, but I'm still mad that he kicked me into touch.' Morgan smiled grimly. 'Oh, I'm *so* going to kick some gorgeous SAS ass.'

Riley nodded. 'That's my girl.'

* * *

Back in London, in his favourite pub, Noah took a listless sip of his beer and looked up as his brothers sat down on the bar stools on either side of him. It seemed that Chris, who was outside taking a call, felt he needed reinforcements for the lecture he intended to dole out. *Wuss.*

Noah sent a look to the door and thought that he could get by Chris if he wanted to. He'd taken on a room full of Colombian thugs—nearly killing one in the process—and won.

Yeah, run away from this conversation like a coward, Fraser—like you did from Morgan. Just to add to the long list of things he'd done lately that he wasn't proud of.

Hamish slapped him on the back and placed their orders for drinks. 'So, let me see if Chris has the story straight. You still haven't spoken to Morgan and apologised?'

No small talk, no lead-up just...*pow!* 'Essentially.'

'You really are a git, big bro',' said Mike, lifting his glass and toasting him. 'Though admittedly it *is* nice to see that you have clay feet. But dumping Morgan...' Mike leaned forward and frowned at him. 'Did you get punched in the head? In other words, *are you freaking insane?*'

Noah lifted his hand to protest and saw that Chris had joined his merry group. 'Thanks,' he said, sarcastically. 'Did they need to know?'

'Sure they need to see their control freak big brother unhinged,' Chris said on a smile.

'I am *not* unhinged,' Noah said through gritted teeth. Miserable and dejected, but still clear-thinking.

'Mmm, that's why you're the model of efficiency at work. *Not.*'

'You talk like a teenage girl,' Noah muttered.

'You're acting like one,' Chris countered.

'And I am not unhinged! Unhinged was what I felt like when I saw that knife to her neck. When I contemplated what life would be without her...' He hadn't meant to add that.

'You're living a life without her,' Mike pointed out. 'And how's *that* working out for you?'

'Shut up, Oprah.'

Bloody awful, but the point was... What was the point? All he knew was that he was scared to love her, scared to lose her, and scared to live this half-life without her in it. He just wanted to go back to his life as it had been before he met her, when he'd been heartless and independent and unemotional.

When life had been easy and uncomplicated. It hadn't quite worked out that way. Yet.

And he really didn't want to have this conversation with his brothers and Chris. There was nothing wrong, in his opinion, with those old-fashioned men-to-men conversations, where they didn't discuss emotions at all. But, no, he had to be saddled with three touchy-feely, new age guys who thought it was perfectly reasonable to discuss his broken heart.

'The least you can do is talk to her,' Hamish suggested.

'Back off,' he growled into his beer.

'Either that or go to my bothy in the Highlands and lick you wounds in private,' Chris suggested.

'Will any of you follow me there and carry on bleating in my ear?' Noah demanded.

They looked at each other, shook their heads. 'Not for a day or two at least.'

'Sold.' Noah slapped his hands on the bar. It was exactly what he needed: time and solitude to think, recover and re-live his time with Morgan.

No, that wasn't right. To *get over* Morgan. Because that was what he had to do, the sensible thing to do.

Ten days from that momentous day—the one that had ended with Noah kicking her out of her life—and she was back in Scotland, Morgan thought, her hands on the wheel of the rental car. She was driving in a country halfway across the world.

James had worked out an agreement at the mine that was complicated and confusing, and the details of which she cared absolutely nothing about. What was important was that everyone was thoroughly convinced that the threat to their well-being was neutralised and her mother and father had come out of hiding thoroughly sick of each other. Her father had disappeared on a trip to investigate a mine in Botswana and her mother had started poking her nose into MI business and, more annoyingly, ball business. Situation normal there.

James and Riley were either snipping at each other, ignoring each other or avoiding each other. Situation... She didn't even know how to categorise their situation...crazy?

The CFT guards—even more robotic than Noah—had gone back to being robotic with someone else and her apartment had become her own again.

Situation so very *not* normal there.

She hated it. She hated the silence and the fact that there was no one to drink wine with, chat with, curl up around at night, make sweet love to in the morning.

She missed him. With every breath she took. But more than anything else she was so steel-meltingly angry with him that he'd just walked away—because she couldn't concentrate on a thing and because her stress levels were stratospheric.

She couldn't design, couldn't make decisions on the ball, couldn't eat, couldn't sleep.

She had a business to run, an important social event to organise, and after she'd given him many, *many* pieces of her mind she'd put him aside and resume her life—go back to normal. She was not going to beg, to tell him she loved him, adored his body, loved his generous, protective spirit. She wouldn't tell him that she'd fallen in love with him eight years ago and never really stopped. *Dammit.*

Morgan felt the familiar cocktail of love and misery and anger churn in her stomach. How dared he throw comments mentioning joy and love at her head and then kick her out of his life? He was the most courageous man she knew except when it came to loving—*keeping!*—her. Well, she wasn't just going to lie down and accept it…

Telling him where to get off and that she was worth taking a chance on were the *only* reasons she was on this godforsaken road in the middle of the Scottish Highlands, probably lost. Again.

Okay, depending on how wretched he was, she might let it slip that she missed him and that she loved him—maybe. Probably.

Morgan yawned and shoved her exhaustion away. She'd landed at Heathrow yesterday, threatened Chris with dismemberment if he didn't tell her where he was and nearly bitten his head off when he'd offered to take her to the bothy close to Auterlochie. She could find it herself, she'd stated grandly, and now she wished she'd taken him up on his offer. Because this place was desolate, and it was getting dark, and there were scary cows with big horns that glared at her from the side of the road.

As night and the temperature fell Morgan saw the glimmer of a stone cottage off the road and wondered if this could possibly be the bothy Noah sometimes escaped to. There were no lights on in the house, and there wasn't any sign of the deep green Land Rover Chris said he used up here.

There was only one way to find out, she thought, bunching her much hated map in her hand and storming up to the front door. After knocking and getting no response she found the door opened to her touch, and she looked around a large room: kitchen at one end, lounge at the other. Through the closed door she presumed there was a bedroom and bathroom. There were battered couches, one that held a jersey draped over its arm. Morgan picked it up and sighed when she inhaled Noah's familiar scent.

The cabin was also ridiculously tidy, and she knew she was in the right place.

She loved him…but she was going to kill him when she

saw him. For making her fall in love with him, for making her chase after him, for being a totally stupid, pathetically scared of commitment, moron *man*.

'What? Not naked this time?' Noah said from the doorway.

Morgan dropped the shirt and whipped around. Her heart bounced and then settled as her eyes drifted over him in the half-light of the cottage.

Kill him...slowly...

'Can you put some lights on?' Morgan asked politely.

'Why?'

'So that I can see your face when I scream at you.'

Morgan blinked as he flicked the switch on the wall next to the door.

Noah walked into the room and shoved his hands into his jeans pockets. Morgan cocked her head at him and saw that there were blue shadows under his eyes and his mouth looked grim. Tense. Possibly scared.

Good. He should be.

'You don't seem very surprised to see me,' Morgan said.

'Chris gave me a heads-up that you were on your way but I expected you hours ago. I was out looking for you. What happened? Did you get lost?'

With that comment he lit the fuse to her temper. 'Of *course* I got lost, you idiot! Lots and lots of times! I forgot to check if there was a GPS when I hired the car! I have dyslexia and I can't read a damn map at the best of times. When I'm sad and stressed and heartbroken and miserable and depressed it's near impossible!'

She scrunched the map into a ball and launched it at his head.

'Tell me how you really feel, Morgs.' Noah struggled to keep his grin from forming.

Morgan looked at him, hurt and shocked. 'You think this is a joke? That the pain you've caused me is funny? I've been travelling for days so that you can *laugh* at me?'

Noah scrubbed his hands over his face. 'No—God, no! Sorry. I didn't mean that. I'm just amazed that you are here; you nearly missed me. I was going to leave in the morning. I'm really, really happy that you *are* here.'

Morgan gave him a stony look. 'Sure you are.. Look, this is stupid. I'm probably very stupid... I'll just go.'

Noah moved to stand in front of the door. 'You're not going anywhere, and you are definitely not driving anywhere in the dark. You might end up in a loch.'

Morgan tried to push him out of the way but she couldn't move his bulk. 'You lost the right to tell me what to do, to protect me, when you kicked me out of your life and sicced those CFT agents on me!'

'I intend to protect you for the rest of your life, if you'll let me.'

Everything in Morgan's body tensed as she looked up into his gorgeous face. The humour had fled and his eyes were deep and serious and radiating truth. And love. And hope. Her heart lurched.

'Come and sit down, Morgan. Please.'

Okay, maybe she could just hear him out...just a little. Morgan allowed Noah to take her hand and she perched on the edge of a couch. Noah pulled the battered coffee table closer to the couch and sat on it, facing her.

'I was—*am*—happy to see you, When I couldn't find you...I thought you'd plunged off the road or crashed some-where. I was considering calling out a search party when I saw your car pull in here. I belted back here, just so relieved that you are okay.'

'Uh-huh.'

'Secondly, I was planning to leave tomorrow. I was going to go home.'

'Back to London.'

'Back to *you*. You are my home, Morgan. You're the place where I want to be.' Noah touched her hand with his fingers. 'I've spent the last week trying to convince myself that I'm better on my own, that I can live without you, that I'm independent and a hard-ass and I don't need anyone. And I don't need *anyone*, Morgs. I just need you. I love you. More than I can express and much more than you will ever know,' he added, his voice saturated with emotion.

'But you sent me away!' Morgan's fist rocketed into his shoulder. 'I loved you, but you sent me away like I was nothing!'

'I sent you away because you were *everything* and I was scared.' Noah gripped her fist and kissed her knuckles. 'I'm stupid when it comes to you—haven't you realised that yet? Do you want me to grovel?'

Morgan sniffed as her head and her heart started pounding with the warm fairy dust sparkles of happiness. 'I can't imagine you grovelling well.'

'True.' Noah kissed her knuckles again and held her eyes. 'I'm sorry that I acted like a jerk.'

'I've been miserable without you. I can't do anything without you,' Morgan grumbled, her fingers on his cheek.

'I know.'

'No, you don't understand. The dyslexia has been really bad—'

'Babe, it's not that. I've also been less than useless at the office...why do you think Chris sent me up here? I couldn't think, hold a reasonable conversation, I forgot meetings and stopped midway through my sentences. I couldn't function without you.' Noah's other hand clasped her face and his thumb drifted over her cheekbone. 'It has nothing to do with the dyslexia and everything to do with the fact that you and I are better together than we are apart.'

'So it seems.'

'Do you remember what you said at Bon Chance? Just before I heard about Michael?'

Morgan nodded.

'I want the whole bang-shoot too—with you. I don't care how many dyslexic kids we have because they will be *our* kids and they will be brilliant in their own ways—just as you are. I will never think anything is lacking in you, or them. Yeah, I'll get frustrated with you—as you will with me—but it will never be caused by your dyslexia. And I will love you, hard, often, passionately, for ever.'

'Oh, Noah. I love you too.' But Morgan thought she should issue one more threat before she allowed pure happiness to envelop her. 'I came here to kick your ass.'

'I'd much prefer to kiss yours.' Noah's curved lips drifted down to hers. Before they touched, he spoke again. 'I don't suppose you packed any of those burlesque corsets, did you? I've been having a few fantasies about them...'

Morgan smiled against his mouth. 'No, you're going to have to earn a corset. You can start by kissing me, soldier.'

'With all my pleasure, Duchess.'

EPILOGUE

Four months later...

IN A CROWD of three thousand people Morgan knew exactly whose hand touched her back—recognised the gentleness in his strong touch. Morgan lifted her solid black mask and smiled at Noah, who'd refused her entreaties to wear a costume as befitting a 1920s burlesque-themed ball or a mask. Then again, nobody could quite pull off a tuxedo like her soldier.

Well, a tuxedo jacket. The lower half of his tuxedo consisted of a kilt in the Fraser tartan, complete with furry sporran.

Noah could pull off a kilt too. Not that she would ever tell him that—she was having far too much fun teasing him about his 'Scottish skirt'.

And naked... Actually nobody could pull off naked as well as Noah could, and as soon as she was done with the ball they were headed for Stellenbosch, where she intended to devote her considerable energies to keeping him naked as much as possible.

Noah placed both his arms around her and held her as they stared down at the crowds below them. The ballroom glittered and heaved with colour, laughter rose and fell, and champagne and other fine spirits flowed. Couples whirled around the dance floor and other guests stood in front of the birdcages and looked at the beautiful pieces of jewellery art.

'Why are you hiding up here on this little balcony by yourself?' Noah asked.

'I just need a break,' Morgan answered. 'Isn't it spectacular, Noah?'

'It is, and you should be proud of yourself. You did this, Duchess. This is all yours and it's fabulous.'

'Well, mine and Ri's. We work well together.'

Morgan rested her head on his chest and stroked his hand with her fingertips. 'By the way, Mum has agreed to using some of the money raised tonight to make a hefty donation to that dyslexic foundation I visited the other day. They want me to sit on their board.'

'Are you going to tell them—tell people about your dyslexia?' Noah asked, turning her to face him.

'I thought...maybe. What do you think?'

'I think that you—apart from the fact that you are the untidiest person alive—are awe-inspiring.' Noah kissed her nose. 'I have something for you.'

'You do? Will I like it?'

Noah looked uncharacteristically serious. 'I hope so. Buying a gift for the Diamond Queen's daughter is a nightmare of epic proportions, and everyone I've spoken to has a different idea about what you like. Riley says one thing, James another—mostly just to take the opposite view to Riley, I think.'

'I have to do something about those two, and soon,' Morgan muttered, her eyes narrowing.

'Hey, concentrate! We're talking about your present. And the angst I've gone through to get it.'

Morgan grinned. 'Sorry. So, what did I do to deserve a present?'

Noah tipped his head in thought. 'Well, you do this little thing with your tongue...'

Morgan blushed. 'Noah! *Jeez!*'

Noah touched her cheek with the back of his knuckle. 'I love you with everything I have and the last months have been crazy exciting.'

'Do you miss London? Your brothers? You've uprooted your life...' Morgan said, a little worried. He'd made huge changes to his life to be with her and she needed to know that he had no regrets.

'We've expanded Auterlochie by opening another branch in the city, and I've moved into a gorgeous flat with a woman who says she loves me and gives me frequent sex. Such a hard thing to do...' Noah said, his eyes laughing at her fears.

Morgan rolled her eyes. *Okay, then.* 'So, about my present...what did you buy me?'

'Not so much buy as...' Noah pulled a box out of his pocket and handed it over. 'We talked about getting married at some point and I wanted to make it official. I know it's not the fanciest or the biggest or the—'

'Shut up, No,' Morgan said, flipping open the lid. Inside, cleaned and sparkling, sat his mother's red beryl ring—the one she hadn't seen since that day in the studio.

Morgan swallowed and put her hand on her chest as she stared at the box in her hand.

He could have had a ring designed by Carl, bought her the flashiest diamond and got down on one knee in front of all these people and proposed, but nothing, Morgan knew, would have had a greater emotional impact on her than receiving his beloved mother's ring.

Morgan pulled it out and handed it back to him.

'You don't want it?' he asked quietly, disappointment in his eyes and voice.

Morgan shook her head, her eyes welling. 'I want you to put it on me. And as you do it,' she added, as Noah picked up her hand and held her ring finger, 'I want to tell you that I'm honoured to wear this ring and that, like her, I will always love you.'

Noah kissed her lips and held her against him, and she felt warm and protected and so very, very loved in his arms.

After a long, emotion-soaked moment he whispered in her ear. 'I'm loving your dress, Duchess.'

She grinned and curtsied. 'Merci.''

She'd had a steam punk green and black corset designed for the evening and teamed it with a black tulle and organza skirt that rode low on her hips and exposed a strip of her belly. It had been worth every penny to see Noah's eyes bug when he'd first caught sight of it.

'I can't wait to get you alone,' Noah said, nuzzling her neck. 'I'm going to have so much fun taking it off you.'

Morgan bent her knees, dipped her hand under his kilt and touched his warm thigh. Her eyes sparkled as she looked up into his face. 'And I'm going to have lots of fun taking *your* skirt off you.'

'It's a kilt!' Noah howled for the umpteenth time that night. 'Respect the kilt!'

Morgan grinned, knowing that her happiness was echoed in his eyes. 'I deeply respect what's under the—'

'Don't say skirt.'

Noah captured her face in his hands and kissed her lips as her hand danced up his thigh.

'Duchess?'

'Yes, soldier?'

'Behave.'

Morgan's eyes laughed at him. 'Absolutely...*not.*'

* * * * *

Mills & Boon® Hardback

April 2014

ROMANCE

A D'Angelo Like No Other	Carole Mortimer
Seduced by the Sultan	Sharon Kendrick
When Christakos Meets His Match	Abby Green
The Purest of Diamonds?	Susan Stephens
Secrets of a Bollywood Marriage	Susanna Carr
What the Greek's Money Can't Buy	Maya Blake
The Last Prince of Dahaar	Tara Pammi
The Sicilian's Unexpected Duty	Michelle Smart
One Night with Her Ex	Lucy King
The Secret Ingredient	Nina Harrington
Her Soldier Protector	Soraya Lane
Stolen Kiss From a Prince	Teresa Carpenter
Behind the Film Star's Smile	Kate Hardy
The Return of Mrs Jones	Jessica Gilmore
Her Client from Hell	Louisa George
Flirting with the Forbidden	Joss Wood
The Last Temptation of Dr Dalton	Robin Gianna
Resisting Her Rebel Hero	Lucy Ryder

MEDICAL

200 Harley Street: Surgeon in a Tux	Carol Marinelli
200 Harley Street: Girl from the Red Carpet	Scarlet Wilson
Flirting with the Socialite Doc	Melanie Milburne
His Diamond Like No Other	Lucy Clark

0314GEN STD HB

Mills & Boon® Large Print

April 2014

ROMANCE

Defiant in the Desert	Sharon Kendrick
Not Just the Boss's Plaything	Caitlin Crews
Rumours on the Red Carpet	Carole Mortimer
The Change in Di Navarra's Plan	Lynn Raye Harris
The Prince She Never Knew	Kate Hewitt
His Ultimate Prize	Maya Blake
More than a Convenient Marriage?	Dani Collins
Second Chance with Her Soldier	Barbara Hannay
Snowed in with the Billionaire	Caroline Anderson
Christmas at the Castle	Marion Lennox
Beware of the Boss	Leah Ashton

HISTORICAL

Not Just a Wallflower	Carole Mortimer
Courted by the Captain	Anne Herries
Running from Scandal	Amanda McCabe
The Knight's Fugitive Lady	Meriel Fuller
Falling for the Highland Rogue	Ann Lethbridge

MEDICAL

Gold Coast Angels: A Doctor's Redemption	Marion Lennox
Gold Coast Angels: Two Tiny Heartbeats	Fiona McArthur
Christmas Magic in Heatherdale	Abigail Gordon
The Motherhood Mix-Up	Jennifer Taylor
The Secret Between Them	Lucy Clark
Craving Her Rough Diamond Doc	Amalie Berlin

0314 GEN STD LP

Mills & Boon® Hardback
May 2014

ROMANCE

The Only Woman to Defy Him	Carol Marinelli
Secrets of a Ruthless Tycoon	Cathy Williams
Gambling with the Crown	Lynn Raye Harris
The Forbidden Touch of Sanguardo	Julia James
One Night to Risk it All	Maisey Yates
A Clash with Cannavaro	Elizabeth Power
The Truth About De Campo	Jennifer Hayward
Sheikh's Scandal	Lucy Monroe
Beach Bar Baby	Heidi Rice
Sex, Lies & Her Impossible Boss	Jennifer Rae
Lessons in Rule-Breaking	Christy McKellen
Twelve Hours of Temptation	Shoma Narayanan
Expecting the Prince's Baby	Rebecca Winters
The Millionaire's Homecoming	Cara Colter
The Heir of the Castle	Scarlet Wilson
Swept Away by the Tycoon	Barbara Wallace
Return of Dr Maguire	Judy Campbell
Heatherdale's Shy Nurse	Abigail Gordon

MEDICAL

200 Harley Street: The Proud Italian	Alison Roberts
200 Harley Street: American Surgeon in London	Lynne Marshall
A Mother's Secret	Scarlet Wilson
Saving His Little Miracle	Jennifer Taylor

0414GEN STD HB

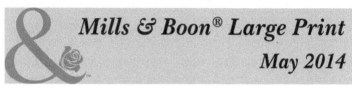

Mills & Boon® Large Print
May 2014

ROMANCE

HISTORICAL

MEDICAL

Discover more romance at

www.millsandboon.co.uk

- ❤ WIN great prizes in our exclusive competitions

- ❤ BUY new titles before they hit the shops

- ❤ BROWSE new books and REVIEW your favourites

- ❤ SAVE on new books with the Mills & Boon® Bookclub™

- ❤ DISCOVER new authors

PLUS, to chat about your favourite reads, get the latest news and find special offers:

- 📘 Find us on facebook.com/millsandboon
- 🐦 Follow us on twitter.com/millsandboonuk
- ❤ Sign up to our newsletter at millsandboon.co.uk